GERALL'S FESTIVUS BRIDE

FAIRELLE BOOK SEVEN

REBEKAH R. GANIERE

Gerall's Festivus Bride © 2018 Rebekah R. Ganiere

All rights reserved. No part of this publication may be reproduced, distributed, or transmitted in any form or by any means, including photocopying, recording, or other electronic or mechanical methods, without the prior written permission of the publisher, except in the case of brief quotations embodied in critical reviews and certain other noncommercial uses permitted by copyright law.

This book is a work of fiction. The names, characters, places and incidents are fictitious and are not to be construed as real in any way. Any resemblance to persons, living or dead, actual events, locales or organizations is coincidental.

Gerall's Festivus Bride © 2018 Rebekah R. Ganiere

ISBN: 978-1-63300-046-9

ISBN: 978-1-63300-050-6

Cover art by Rebekah R. Ganiere

vwzdesigns.com

DEDICATION

For the Outcasts, the Forgotten, the Unloved and the Weird - Welcome to my Tribe!

NEWSLETTER

To claim your Two FREE Books and find out more about Rebekah R. Ganiere and her other Upcoming Releases You can Go Here: www.RebekahGaniere.com/Newsletter

Fairelle
N
W
E
S
Tanah Darah
Shaidan
Wolvenglen
Daemon Wastelands
Sage's Hideout
Rift
Ruins
Snow's Cottage
Volkzene
Westfall
Belle's Cottage
Gwyn Manor
Mortain
Abandoned Castle
Ville DeFee
Zelle's Tower
Draak Land
Ryna's Lake
Wizard Towers
Vedenalla

PROLOGUE

PEREUM, FAIRELLE YEAR 200

In the year 200, in the city of Pereum, the heart of Fairelle, King Isodor lay on his deathbed. With all of Fairelle united under his banner, his four sons vied for the crown. One by one the brothers called forth a djinn named Xereus from Shaidan, the daemon realm, to grant a single wish. But Xereus tricked the brothers, twisting their wishes.

The eldest wished to forever be bloodthirsty in battle, and was thus transformed into a Vampire. The second wished for the unending loyalty of his men, and was turned into a Werewolf. The third asked for the ability to manipulate the elements of Fairelle; he became physically weak but mighty in magick, a Fae. And the last asked to rule the sea. A Nereid.

When the king died, each brother took a piece of Fairelle for himself and waged war for control of the rest. Xereus, having been called forth so many times, tore a rift between his daemonic plane and Fairelle, allowing thousands of daemons to pour into Pereum.

Years upon years of bloody warring went by with all races fighting for control and eventually the daemons gained dominion of the heart of Fairelle. Realizing that all lands would soon fall into the daemons' control, the High Elders of the Fae and the Mages from the south, combined their magicks to seal the rift. The daemons were banished back to their own plane, but Pereum was wiped off the map in the process, leaving only charred waste behind forever known as The Daemon Wastelands.

Upon the day of the rift closing, a Mage soothsayer prophesied of the healing of Fairelle. Over the next thousand years the races continued to war against each other, waiting for the day when the ancient prophesies would begin.

Eight prophesies, a thousand years old, to unite the lands and heal Fairelle.

CHAPTER ONE

WESTFALL, FAIRELLE - EARLY FALL, 1213 A.D. (AFTER DAEMONS)

Gerall smiled and ran his blade through the vampire's neck. Its eyes widened before he turned to ash. Breathing a contented sigh, Gerall coughed. *Damn.* It had been so long since he'd fought vampires that he'd forgotten to take a step back, so as not to get corpse dust in his mouth. The taste of charred wood coated his tongue, sucking all moisture from it. He tried to spit, but couldn't produce any saliva.

"Is that all of them?" Jamen called, crunching through the thick leaves toward them.

"I think so," replied Erik.

Gerall glanced around, and even in the dark, he could make out the bright yellow, orange, and burgundy leaves on the autumn trees. He wiped his mouth on the back of his sleeve and shook ash from his unruly hair. It had been almost a year since he and his brothers had gone out on the hunt, and if truth be told, he missed it.

Ever since Sage and Snow had taken over ruling Tanah Darah, there'd been little for the brothers to do. While going out and hunting vampires had once been a nightly ritual for them, they now did little more than engage in occasional sport with the dissenters.

The tracking late at night, racing on his steed while the world slept, being with his brothers. Forgetting their fractured family. It soothed his lonely heart.

He didn't miss the broken fingers or the gashes that needed stitches, having to replace his glasses every month, or living a double life. He missed the camaraderie of his brothers. He missed being together. He missed… His family.

Though life and happiness finally filled the house again, Snow had been gone for well over a year, and no one could replace her. Jamen's and Flint's marriages and babies they produced blessed all of them, but things were not the same without Snow and Kellan. Even Dax, Belle, and little Chloe's absences left a hole.

"I do not understand why they bother trying to come down here and hunt. They know we'll come after them." Jamen mounted his horse.

"Guess it's in their nature. To hunt for food as opposed to have it sitting willingly at the table waiting to be eaten." Gerall took off his glasses and wiped them on his tunic.

"Did you see the girl?" Erik sheathed his sword and grabbed the reins of his horse.

"No," replied Jamen. "If she was among them, she fled."

"She wasn't." Gerall wiped his blade on his pants. "There were only five."

Erik shook his head. "Damn. All right. Let's head back to the manor house. I'll clean up and go to Tanah Darah to inform Snow."

"That vampire girl has been gone for long enough–"

"She's most likely dead." Hass and Ian strode to their horses and hopped into the saddle.

"I promised Snow and Sage I would locate the girl. I, at least, need to find out what happened to her." A hard edge crept into Erik's voice.

"What does one girl matter?" asked Jamen.

Erik's expression darkened. "I made a vow."

"And what about your vow as Lord?" asked Jamen. "Tomorrow is Westfall day. The first day in the week-long Autumn Festivus. You need to meet with the magistrate. With enemies all around meaning to undermine our position, we need to be present more than ever."

"I'll go." Gerall slid his sword into its holster. "I need to go into town anyway to pick up a few things. Jamen, Scarlet, Flint, Zelle, and the children can accompany me. It would be good for Westfall to see how our family has grown. Let them know that we aren't going anywhere."

"What?" said Ian.

"We're not invited?" asked Hass.

Erik nodded. "Gerall's right. He can go in my place, and the rest of you can enjoy Festivus. I'll head back out to find the girl and will return within the week."

Jamen shook his head. "You and your damned honor."

"I call the bath when we get back," said Hass.

"Not if I get there first," replied Ian.

The two kicked their steeds and sped off.

Gerall smiled to himself. He missed this.

The group piled through the solar door to the manor house and the smell of beef stew and warm rolls struck Gerall. He gave thanks for Zelle and Scarlet and the way they cared for all of them, though they didn't have to.

"How did it go?" Flint entered the solar, carrying his daughter Lucia. Without his glasses on, his sight was all but nonexistent. But over the passing months, Gerall had seen Flint become more and more comfortable without it. Flint knew every inch of the manor house and rarely bumped into anything anymore. Especially with Loca always hovering around or perched on his shoulder.

Gerall's gut clenched, and he studied Flint's face, but there appeared to be no resentment at Erik telling him to stay home instead of joining them on the hunt.

"We got rid of them," said Jamen.

"Did you find that girl?"

"No," replied Erik. "I need to see Snow and find out what we do next."

Flint nodded. "Before you do, there's someone you need to see."

The brothers looked at each other.

"He's waiting in the dining hall."

They walked with Flint through the front hallway.

Erik pushed open the door and Gerall's brow furrowed.

"King Adrian." Jamen advanced and offered Adrian his hand.

The wolves never left Wolvenglen to go anywhere but

Volkzene. For Adrian to visit, meant the news couldn't be good.

"Is something wrong?" asked Erik.

Adrian stood, towering over all of them except Flint. "One of my wolves went missing. We are still looking for him"

"Missing?" asked Gerall.

"His name is Fendrick. He went out with his children to play in the woods, and the children came back, but he did not."

"Is it possible he ran off?" asked Flint.

"No. Fendrick isn't like my other wolves. He's… unstable. His only pleasure is being with his wife and children. He would never leave them."

"I remember him," said Jamen. "Hanna's husband. Tall, thin man. Eyes like a cornered rabbit."

"Yes. And if you remember, I couldn't send Hanna with you to help Scarlet's aunt because of his instability. He would never leave of his own accord. And especially never leave his young. It's not possible."

"What can we do?" asked Erik.

"I tracked his scent to the edge of Westfall, but then I lost it."

"He came here?" asked Flint.

"Not of his own accord." Adrian ran his hands through his hair. "I don't want to cause any problems, but I would like your permission to search Westfall. Not intrusively, just look about the town and see if I can pick up a scent."

"Of course," said Erik. "Anything you need."

"Would it be all right if I spent the night with you?"

"Our home is your home," said Jamen.

Adrian nodded. "I thank you."

"Why don't we get you something to eat? Tomorrow is Westfall Day, and there is going to be a festival. All of the town folk will be out. It will help you blend in better."

Adrian nodded. "Again. I thank you."

"I'll be heading to Tanah Darah within the hour," said Erik. "I'll let Sage and Snow know of the missing wolf in case they've seen or heard anything."

"Come on." Jamen clapped Adrian on the back. "Let's get you fed and find you a bed."

Adrian strode out with Jamen.

"First a vampire missing, now a werewolf," said Erik.

"Whatever is going on, it can't be good," replied Flint.

"It's got to be connected to the murder of the doctor and his wife and Scarlet's aunt. And the conspiracy against us being the ruling family of Westfall," said Gerall.

"Sir Malcolm and his sons aren't back, are they?" asked Flint.

Gerall shook his head. "No. Someone would have notified us if they'd returned. And Jamen would have mentioned it."

"Let's not jump to conclusions quite yet," said Erik. "I'll go to Snow's. You lot go with Adrian to town tomorrow. Feel things out. See what you hear. Hass and Ian can even ride by Malcolm's to make sure he, Edward and Lyden haven't returned. But if this is connected to the death of the doctor, and Scarlet's aunt, it can't be good for any of us."

"Agreed," said Flint.

Erik gave Gerall a tight smile and then headed out of

the dining hall. A flutter of anxiety lodged in Gerall's gut. What would someone want with a vampire girl and an unstable werewolf? Hell, why did someone want to hurt his family?

"There will be blood," said Flint, breaking the silence. "I can guarantee you that."

"Let's hope not," replied Hass.

"Because there's a good chance if that's true, it's going to be innocent blood," finished Ian.

CHAPTER TWO

Gerall reined his black steed to a stop and hopped to the ground in front of the Westfall stable. He brushed the light layer of dust off his shoulders and scanned the street. Every shop window held a bouquet of wildflowers and over every entrance hung a bow of white sage, burdock, and blackberry leaf, symbolizing the cleansing of autumn and soon the slumber of winter. The scent of cinnamon, pumpkin and crisp apples clung to the air.

He smiled, letting the smells and freshness invade him. Seeing the vibrant colors paint his homeland and the happiness and gratitude that people bestowed upon each other in the beginnings of the holiday season, lightened his soul. He prayed the upcoming year would bring with it joy and prosperity to his family, as well.

Behind him, Flint, Adrian, and Jamen dismounted their horses as Hass pulled the family carriage that hadn't been used in close to five years up alongside. He and Ian hopped from the front and opened the door.

"Lords Gwyn." A man rushed toward Gerall. "How wonderful to see you. You haven't been to town in quite some time."

Gerall tried to remember the man's name. He had always relied on Erik and Snow to tell him who people were. He could name every flower and fauna in most of Fairelle, yet he couldn't remember the name of anyone outside his own family.

"Yes, we've been quite busy lately." Flint squinted behind his red glasses and took his son, Marcus, from Zelle's arms.

Jamen plucked two-year-old Kellan from Scarlet and held his hand out to her so she could exit the carriage. Her form rounded with the new life she carried once more. She swore this one would be a girl, which Gerall knew was Jamen's greatest hope.

"I heard Lady Snow married a prince from a different kingdom. How nice for her." The man smiled and took the reins from Gerall, patting the horse on the neck.

Gerall's mouth dried, but he smiled. "She is quite happy."

"Wonderful." His eyes turned to Adrian. "And you must be…"

"This is Adrian," said Flint. "A distant cousin of ours from the Volkzene area."

"Volkzene. My, I don't think I've ever met anyone from there before. I thought they kept to themselves."

"We tend to mostly. Unless business pulls us southward."

Adrian scanned the street in broad sweeps as he breathed deeply.

"Well, welcome to Westfall. I'll take your horse in and get him brushed and fed."

"The carriage seemed a bit bumpy on the way in," said Hass.

"Can you find someone to look to the wheels?" finished Ian.

The man nodded. "Of course, M'lords. I won't keep you any longer. Have a blessed day."

Gerall waved and stared at the man, hoping the name would cross his mind, but it didn't. The bell of the town church chimed ten.

"I must go. I'll be late for the meeting."

Hass and Ian smiled. "Well, you have fun with all that duty. We'll think of you while we're off feasting in the inn."

"I could go," offered Flint. "I've been doing it for close to a year."

Gerall clapped his older brother's large shoulder. "That's all right. You have fun with Zelle and the children. I won't be long. I'll meet you for lunch."

"You should make it quick," replied Jamen. "With Hass and Ian in town, there may not be any left."

Adrian's gaze darted back and forth. "I'm going to see if I can pick up the scent."

"If you do, let us know," said Flint. "We can't afford any fights today."

Adrian nodded. "I won't do anything without consulting you first."

Gerall straightened his tunic and pushed his glasses up

his nose. He strode from the group and across the dirt thoroughfare toward the magistrate's office. He abhorred politics. But he abhorred anyone trying to tarnish his family even more, and he would be damned if he'd let anyone harm any of them.

In the short and uneventful meeting, the magistrate handed over the list of town indiscretions he'd taken care of, along with the rents and a short list of people seeking to speak with Erik. They'd gone over the schedule for the week of festivities and then set a date for the next meeting to be before the Yuletide celebration and the New Year.

Gerall strolled from shop to shop, watching as each prepared their wares for Festivus. Browsing the town and being out of the manor house eased his loneliness and made his heart lighter. But as he looked at the faces of the townsfolk, he found himself wondering what they would think of the Gwyn family if they knew all the secrets tucked deep behind the heavy manor doors. Who would still nod, bow, curtsy or send well wishes at the sight of him? And how many would curse them, spit or side with those trying to rip Westfall from their ruling grip? Too many, he feared— too many.

Gerall stopped in the glassmaker's shop to say hello. Then he traveled to the apothecary to restock his supplies and show them a few samples he'd picked up in Snow's garden in Tanah Darah, to see if they could identify them.

By noon, his stomach growled loudly, and the smell of fresh bread and sweet rolls pulled him down the street. He passed the cobbler, the candle maker, and the butcher as if possessed and didn't stop until he reached his destination.

The bakery window overflowed with every delight a person could imagine. The outside of the shop had been decorated with beautiful bright colors. Pastries and cakes, cookies, and loaves of bread of every shape and size filled his view. Times had obviously been good to the baker and his family. In looking about the town, he realized he couldn't see any portion that lacked prosperity of one sort or another. Again, the edgy sword of dread hung low against his neck, making him wonder with so much prosperity why someone conspired against his family.

"Lord Gwyn."

Gerall turned at the sound of his name. The magistrate wobbled over, his jovial, round face barely coming up to Gerall's chest. "Hello again, Magistrate Jopin."

Jopin's gaze traveled into the bakery. "Getting a bite to eat?"

Gerall eyed the window of the shop. "I don't remember the bakery having so many choices last I was in town."

"It's changed quite a bit in the past month or so. Anyway, I forgot to ask you if you'd do me the honor of dining at my home tonight?"

"Oh no," said Gerall. "I couldn't possibly impose on your lovely wife. Snow would kill me if she knew I'd shown up without letting your wife know first. She always called it bad manners."

"I'm sure my wife would be just fine with it."

"Thank you," said Gerall. "Perhaps another time. I'm just going to grab something right quick, and then I'll be joining my family for the rest of the day. It is wonderful to be able to come to Festivus. We have been so greatly blessed this year past. What with three new Gwyns born and another on the way."

"Quite wonderful, indeed. And how are things with you all, now that Snow has left you?"

"Not quite as clean, unfortunately. And Snow was an amazing cook. But having Scarlet, Zelle and the children help to make up for it." Gerall swallowed the lump in his throat. Over the past year, he'd spent as much time in Tanah Darah as he had in Westfall. With all the new family members that had joined them, he didn't quite know where he fit anymore.

"See her much, do you?"

Gerall studied the magistrate's face for signs that he might be probing for something deeper. But the man revealed no ulterior motive.

He and his brothers hadn't made any formal announcement of her engagement, and there'd been no town celebration. The only reason anyone knew Snow had even gone was that soon after her wedding, Jamen had resumed his late nights at the tavern, which had mercifully stopped since Scarlet had returned.

"Every chance we get." Gerall smiled.

"Magistrate Jopin?" a woman called from across the way.

"I'll let you go," said Gerall. "See you tomorrow when the festivities begin."

"Very good," said the magistrate. "I hope that your family will be there to begin the ceremony with the cleansing of the wishing well and the pronouncement of the Festival Queen."

"Of course." Gerall gave a small bow. "We would be honored."

Jopin stepped away from Gerall and hurried as fast as his little legs could take him, toward the woman calling to him.

Gerall opened the bakery door and stepped inside. A chime sounded, and the smell of sugar and yeast filled his nose, making his stomach growl again. All around him, pastries filled baskets and jars and containers. His mouth watered at the sight. He walked around, looking over the various sundries. Gerall hadn't seen even half the variety of pastries in the store before. The magistrate was right; the bakery had changed.

After several minutes of browsing, no one appeared. Strange. He'd never seen the shop without the baker behind the counter.

"Hello?" Gerall called. "Mr. Lenter?" He couldn't have gone far. The old baker's living quarters were attached to the back of the shop.

Gerall glanced at the fabric curtain that separated the kitchen from the front. Perhaps something had happened. Maybe Mr. Lenter had fallen.

"Mr. Lenter," he called again, walking around the counter to the curtained-off area. He pushed the curtain aside slightly and looked into the space beyond. Four large ovens burned hot, warming the room and providing its only light.

"Hello?" Gerall stepped beyond, and the floorboard

squeaked. A girl appeared suddenly from around a corner, and her eyes widened.

"I'm sorry, were you calling? I didn't hear you." She wiped her hands on the apron front of her dress, pressing it down.

Gerall swallowed. "Are you alright?"

The girl advanced on him, forcing him to back out of the kitchen.

"Yes, thank you. I was just in the house."

Gerall moved to the bakery floor. The girl stepped up to the counter, and the light struck her bright emerald eyes. Her peachy skin paled against dark, burnt umber hair. Lush, tempting lips accentuated high cheekbones and almond-shaped eyes. He stared at her for several seconds. When he didn't speak, she cleared her throat, and her cheeks flushed a deep shade of rose. Something about her held an exotic quality that he'd never seen before. The way her eyes turned up just slightly in the corners— the perfect bow of her upper lip.

"Can I help you get something?" she finally asked, meeting his gaze.

Gerall shook his head, and his cheeks heated. What was wrong with him? It wasn't like he'd never seen a girl before.

"Sorry." He coughed, trying to get his voice to work. "Yes. Is Mr. Lenter here?"

Her eyes grew sad. "I'm sorry, he's not. He died a few months back. Is there perhaps something I can do for you? I'm his daughter, Eloa."

"Eloa? Little Eloa. It's not possible. Just a few years ago, you were so…"

"Young?" She laughed. "The last time I saw you, Lord Gwyn, you weren't half so tall."

Gerall laughed. "No need for formality. I'm Gerall, the third oldest. My brothers Erik and Flint are the ones people show respect to, not me. I'm just Gerall."

He couldn't even remember the last time he'd been in the bakery. Was it five years? Six? He could have sworn that Eloa was no more than maybe ten at that time, but now... Now she appeared a full-grown woman of twenty.

Eloa cocked her head to the side. "Why shouldn't people show you the same respect as your brothers? You have the same parents, do you not?"

Gerall's brow creased. "Well, yes, but I'm not the oldest."

"Does that make you less of a man somehow?" Her question came out honest, and her eyes remained full and round like a doe's.

Gerall pushed his glasses up his nose. "I suppose not."

She laughed. The sound twinkled around the store and warmed Gerall's heart. "I'm sorry. I didn't mean to embarrass you. What can I get you today, Lord Gwyn?"

What an intriguing creature she'd grown into. He could swear that just a few years prior she'd been playing with a doll in the corner. But with curves and dips in all the right places, hypnotic gentle eyes, and a mischievously bewitching mouth that begged to be kissed. She was nothing short of enchanting. And very much no longer a little girl.

Gerall cleared his throat. "I needed to get some lunch and some bread and some pastries to take home as well."

"Here." She pulled a puffy pastry from a basket. "I just

made these. They're filled with goose and cranberries. Eat that while I fetch your other items."

Gerall took the leaf-shaped pastry from Eloa and sniffed it. It warmed his hand, and his mouth watered. He'd never smelled anything like it. He took a bite and let out an audible moan.

Eloa smiled. "I'm glad you like it."

The taste exploded on his tongue. The pastry was crusty on the outside but soft on the inside. The goose and cranberries melted in his mouth with spices that he couldn't identify.

She pulled two loaves of bread out of a basket and set them in a bag. "Are you fond of any particular pastry, or would you just like a variety?"

"I have to say. I loved your father's baked goods, but yours are… incredible." He didn't have the words. "I'll take a dozen of these." Gerall took another huge bite. "And I'm going to need a half dozen loaves of bread. Anything with seeds you might have, as well as gooseberries. My brothers are big eaters."

"How many Gwyn lords are there?" Eloa put more bread into the sack.

"Seven—" Gerall stopped cleared his tightening throat. "There were seven of us. Our youngest brother, Kellan, passed a year ago."

She stopped and turned to him. "I'm so sorry." Her eyes misted. "I know how hard it is to lose someone you love." Silence hung between them for a moment, and then she turned back to the bread rack. "Your brother, Kellan, was always a sweet boy."

Boy? Surely Kellan had been older than Eloa.

"I should be used to losing loved ones by now. Mother and father died several years ago and now Kellan, and with Snow gone—" He stared at the counter, the feelings of sadness and loss quickly mounting inside. They never spoke about Kellan's death.

"Hey?"

Gerall looked up to find Eloa next to him. She placed her hand on his arm, making his skin suddenly light with interest. The way her emerald eyes gazed up at him made his heart gallop.

"People move on from this life and into the life to come. That doesn't mean they leave us; it just means our relationship becomes different. We may no longer see them daily, but they're still with us."

Gerall sucked in a deep breath, trying to clear his head. Why did she make him feel like he was back in school and flirting with the prettiest girl in the class? Something, admittedly, he'd never dared to do.

"Thank you." He stepped away and turned toward the window.

Flint, Zelle, Scarlet, Jamen and the children browsed the toymaker's shop across the way.

"I should get going. My brothers are waiting."

"Of course. I'm sorry." Eloa's voice held a note of sadness. "I didn't mean to keep you."

Gerall finished his food. "Your baking is exceptional. Would you mind if I held a weekly standing order for the same as today's?"

"That would be most agreeable and welcome," she said.

"Business has slowed a bit since father died. There's been talk of another bakery opening."

Gerall smiled. "Well, I'll be sure to let everyone know just how wonderful your shop is."

"Thank you, Lord Gwyn. You are welcome here any time." She picked up the sacks and walked toward the door. "I can take these to the stable for you if you wish. So, you don't have to carry them."

"Oh, that won't be necessary. I can do it."

He reached for the bags, but she held on to them.

"It's no bother."

His hand rested on hers and for a moment, their eyes connected. Tremors of desire washed through him. His fingers lingered a moment too long, and then he slid them away.

He reached into his tunic for his purse. "What do I owe you?"

"Oh, um…" Eloa looked down at the sacks.

"Here." He removed three gold pieces.

"No, no. That's way too much." Eloa pushed at his hand.

"Of course." Gerall put one of the gold pieces back. "I'll tell you what. I'll give you two—" He put up his hand to stop her protests. "I'll give you two, and you can add anything you think makes up the difference to my sack next week. How about that?"

Eloa bit her lip, and she eyed the money. "I would need to add half the shop to the bag to make up that much."

"Then keep the rest for yourself and buy something nice at the Festivus Festival tomorrow."

"Will you be coming?" Her cheeks flushed, and she pressed her lips together as if wishing to recant her question.

"Will you have a booth with more pastries?"

A broad smile played across her lips and crinkled the corners of her eyes. "Yes."

"Then, I'll be there."

She chuckled. "I will see you tomorrow then."

Gerall reached for the sacks again, and she pulled them away.

"But I insist on taking these to the stable for you."

Such independence. He liked that. He fought for something more to say, some way to engage her longer, but he'd detained her enough already. It wasn't proper for him to intrude on her time so much. She had things to do, and most likely a dozen handsome suitors vying for affection. He was just the third in line to a Lordship that would, gods willing, never fall on his shoulders. Aside from living in a warm, comfortable home with his family, he didn't have much to offer.

He placed the money in Eloa's palm. She shoved the gold into her apron pocket and headed toward the door. Gerall beat her to it and opened it for her.

They stepped out into the sunshine, and she looked up and closed her eyes, bathing in the light. He wanted to say something funny and endearing, but his brain wouldn't work at the sight of her. She opened her eyes again and smiled.

"I don't get out enough during the daylight." Her gaze traveled behind him and her expression fell.

Gerall glanced over his shoulder and found two men leaning against the window of the butcher shop, watching them. He scanned the men. Beefy and menacing. Their stances belied that of a casual air, but they obviously waited for something— him perhaps, or Eloa. Their long coats no doubt held at least one knife, if not two. He turned, and Eloa's gaze hit the ground. The hairs at the base of his neck stood on end.

"Are they bothering you?"

"What?" Her head snapped up. "No. I'm fine. I just… I'll see you tomorrow, Lord Gwyn." Eloa gave a small curtsy and tore off down the street.

His gaze traveled back to the two men. One of them caught Gerall's stare and nudged the other. They nodded to Gerall and ducked into the butcher's shop.

When Gerall sucked in a deep breath, he realized he gripped his dagger tightly. He hadn't even remembered moving his hand. The men made Gerall's skin crawl. He looked down the roadway for Eloa, but she'd disappeared.

"Gerall," called Hass.

"Are you coming?" Ian finished.

He swung his gaze to the butcher shop. For all the beauty and prosperity of their township, something in Westfall wasn't quite right. A danger that lurked under the surface, bubbling and churning like a pot ready to boil over.

Adrian rendezvoused with them, having found nothing that led to Fendrick.

"I'll retrace my steps north and see if I can pick up the trail again," he said.

"We're here if you need us," replied Jamen.

"And we'll keep our eyes and ears open as well to see if we can find out more," Gerall assured him.

"I thank you again. And pray mercy on whomever took Fendrick. If they have him chained, they are safe. But when he gets loose… Well, then gods help anyone that stands between him and returning home."

CHAPTER THREE

Eloa peeked around the corner from the stable toward her shop. Lord Gerall stared at Charlie and Trent. She held her breath as a minute passed, and then the men disappeared into the butcher shop. Lord Gerall removed his hand from under his cloak, where she decided he must have a hidden weapon.

He pushed his glasses up the bridge of his nose and then ran his hand through his curly hazelnut colored hair. The only man she'd ever met taller than Gerall was his brother Flint. He wasn't as stalky the rest of his brothers, but he sported broad shoulders and long, lean legs. His kind coffee-colored eyes and gentle disposition had appealed to her for as long as she could remember, but something told her he knew how to handle himself in a fight. Soft-spoken and polite, his very nature attested to a silent strength that he only used when necessary. Though it had been over five years, she'd recognized him instantly, and had fought every girlish instinct to keep her delight hidden at seeing him.

It'd been the first day of Festivus five years ago, and his father had just finished the cleansing ceremony. All the other children had thrown a haypence into the well and made a wish, but she'd had none. He couldn't have been more than eighteen or nineteen at the time. He'd offered her a coin and then asked her what she'd wished for. So embarrassed by his attention, she'd run off and hid in the bakery window until he, his brothers, and sister had continued down to the green.

She watched him now with the same rapt fasciation that she had those few years ago. She'd heard the rumors around Westfall about the Gwyn family. But watching him meet up with several of his brothers and their families, they looked nothing like what she'd imagined. Far from broken and unfit to lead, they appeared jovial and happy. A family. A real family. Her gut clenched. The one thing she'd always dreamed of.

Eloa looked both ways and then hitched up her skirt and ran back to her store. Refusing to look toward the butcher's, her hands trembled by the time she reached her shop door. She slammed the door and locked it. Trying to control her racing heartbeat, she wrapped her arms around herself.

For months, Charlie and Trent had been nosing around trying to get Eloa to pay a protection fee. They'd never been able to intimidate her father, but lately, the pair of thugs had been making a regular appearance in the shop. Every time they'd come, she'd refused to pay, and every time they'd left carrying half of her baked goods for the day with them.

Eloa refused to go to the Magistrate for the same reason her father had. There were worse things that could happen to her if the law became involved.

"Eloanya?"

Eloa's head lifted at the sound of her father's voice. "Coming, Papa." She looked out the front window once more to find the men back outside watching her. She checked the lock again and then strode to the back room. How would they make money if she had to lock her doors half the time?

The kitchen fires warmed her as she walked past them and into the large adjoining room fit with two beds, a table, and chairs. Her father sat on the larger of the two beds. A worn, cornflower blue comforter pushed to the side.

"Eloa darling, is everything okay? I heard the door slam."

She put on her best smile. "It was just a gust of wind." She sat on the edge of the bed and patted her father's back. The oven explosion that had almost taken his life had been no accident. She was sure of it. His hands, arms, and feet remained wrapped in the makeshift bandages she changed daily. His wounds weren't recovering properly because she couldn't get him a real healer without exposing that he still lived. The best she could do was keep them clean and moist.

"Did I hear a customer today?" he asked.

"Yes." She picked up the hairbrush from the small nightstand and brushed at his long silvery hair. "Lord Gwyn stopped by and picked up some goods."

"Lord Gwyn? The eldest?"

"No. Gerall. The third eldest."

He turned to her. “The one with the glasses?”

Eloa nodded. “That’s him.”

“He’s a nice boy. But you need to marry someone with more inheritance. It will keep you safe.”

Eloa pulled her father’s hair into a leather strap and tugged down the sides to cover his ears. “I shall marry for love. Like you.”

He shook his head. “You must find a man, a powerful man. Only then will you and your children be protected here in Westfall.”

“And who will protect you?”

“All I want is to see you find happiness and then I’ll return to Ville DeFee to be buried with my kin.”

Eloa hugged her father, trying to hold back her tears. “Don’t say that. You still have years and years ahead of you.”

Sadness clouded her father’s face. “I should have gone back to my homeland after your mother’s death instead of hiding here. If I’d not been so selfish when you were young, and I’d sent you to live with my mother, no one would have known that you weren’t full-blooded fae. You have their beauty and power.”

“You know I don’t wish for that. I have always been happy here. And who would I have become had I been raised in a society so judgmental of those without magick? They’d never have let me see you again.”

He gave her a sad smile. She knew her magick brought her father both pride and pain since his had all but completely faded by the time he’d met and married her mother.

Eloa's father sighed. "It's too late, anyway. My mother is dead, as are my brothers. There is no one left there to care for you even if I did send you. I'm sorry, my daughter. Sorry for keeping you here. For not giving you brothers and sisters to comfort you when I'm gone. For not giving you the life I should have."

Eloa's heart squeezed. She had no interest in going to live in Ville DeFee. Her place was with her father in Westfall. The home where she'd spent her life learning magic and writing and reading and baking. The area that smelled of sugar and cinnamon. Her place. Home.

"Look." Eloa dug in her pocket and pulled out the gold coins. "Lord Gerall paid for the baked goods and told me that he wants a weekly order."

"Two gold? Did he buy the whole shop?"

"He tried to give me three, but I refused. He said that I could give him extra goods next week."

"You could give him a day's worth of goods for that price." Her father's gaze stayed on the coins for a moment. "Take one of them and put it in a safe place. You never know when you might need it."

Eloa's brow furrowed. "What could I possibly need it for?"

"It's time we started looking toward your future. This shop isn't where I want you to spend the rest of your days. You put that gold away and save it. And from now on, anything he gives you over the asking price, you put somewhere safe."

"But father—"

"I won't be disobeyed in this. Too long, you've waited on

me. Nursed me and let life pass you by because of my sins. But no more. You will no longer tend to me as a burden. I will do for myself or not at all."

For the first time since the accident, a determination lit in her father's eyes that gave her hope.

"If that is what you wish, Papa."

"It is. I am your past, and you have a long future ahead of you. You need to look to it."

Eloa stared at the gold pieces. Her future. She'd never thought of having a future before. Lord Gerall's kind, handsome face flashed into her mind. His strong jawline and ears that stuck out just a little too much made her smile. Somehow, between the way he looked at her and his kindness, she almost thought a future of her own might be possible.

Eloa spent the next several hours tidying up the shop and making a to-do list for the following day. She had much to accomplish. She'd already gotten together her table and baskets, and she magicked up a beautiful banner to hang from the front of the table. She had just begun pulling out crates to pack up various glass plates when Armie stopped by and bought two loaves of bread. After him, the glassmaker stopped in for a few cookies and a pie for his wife. Both asked if she'd be attending the festivities the following day. Eloa could only attribute the customers to Lord Gerall. His kindness truly knew no bounds.

She was just closing up when Magistrate Jopin entered. Eloa licked her lips, and her gaze shifted to the curtain, separating her from the hut behind the store.

"Good evening, Magistrate," said Eloa. "How nice of you to stop by. Would you like a cup of tea?"

"No, no thank you, my dear. It's my wife's birthday tomorrow, and I had hoped you might have something for the occasion."

Eloa's heart skipped. If she could impress the Magistrate, it might mean even more business. "Of course." She smiled. "Is there something specific your wife likes?"

"She's very fond of draepons, but they are so hard to find this time of season."

"I have some preserved draepons in reserve."

His eyes widened in surprise. "Do you? How many do you have?"

Eloa's heart sank a bit. She didn't want to sell him her draepons; she wanted to sell him her baked goods. "Not too many," she lied. "But enough, maybe for a few things." If she was going to have to sell them to him, she wasn't going to sell them all.

"Oh." His face fell. "That's too bad. I'm throwing her a celebration this weekend, and I had hoped to order several cakes as well as pastries. Of course, I'd also need some rolls and such as well to feed say, twenty people?"

Eloa swallowed hard. Pastries and cakes and bread enough for twenty people was an incredible order.

"But if you can't do it—"

"I can," she blurted. Eloa cleared her throat. "What I mean is, yes, I think I should have enough for that, if I don't overdo it on the draepons."

The Magistrate wagged his finger. "I don't want you to

spread it too thin though. I don't want to be perceived as cheap."

"Of course not, Magistrate."

"So, I can count on you for the baked goods?"

"Absolutely." She tried hard not to beam. Twenty people. Twenty, *influential* people, no doubt.

"Splendid. Then I shall have them picked up Friday, say around four?"

"I would be happy to deliver them free of charge."

"Then we are agreed. I'll pay you when the items are delivered."

Eloa nodded. "Thank you, Sir. You won't be sorry."

"I'm sure I won't." He turned to leave and then turned back. "Oh, I almost forgot. Gerall said that you had some goose and cranberry pastries that were heavenly. Do you think I might…"

"They're right here." Eloa showed him to the basket. "Feel free to help yourself."

"Are you sure?" He gazed at them and licked his lips.

"I insist," she replied.

He smiled. "Thank you, my dear." The Magistrate reached in and plucked the remaining three pastries from the basket. He shoved two into his cloak and the third he bit into immediately. His eyes widened in surprise. "Remarkable. This is truly delicious," he said through full cheeks.

"Thank you."

"Your father never made anything half so good. Where did you learn to make these?"

Goosebumps ran up her arms, and she hoped her father

hadn't heard the unkind remark. "It's an old family secret from my mother's side."

The Magistrate laughed. "Well, if she'd given it to your father, he'd have been a wealthy man before he died."

Eloa's throat tightened. "Perhaps he would have."

"If I were you, I'd make up dozens and dozens of these to sell tomorrow at the festival. I'm sure they will go faster than rabbit stew." The Magistrate wiped his mouth on his sleeve before sticking his hand out to her. "I wish you goodnight. And look forward to having more of these tomorrow."

Eloa shivered at the thought of having to shake the hand of a man who'd just shoved food into his mouth and then wiped his mouth on his sleeve. "Goodnight." She shook his hand quickly and then pulled her palm away. Her fingers twitched with the need to wash.

Opening the door, he dug into his pocket and pulled out a second pastry. He'd bit it in half by the time the door closed. Eloa locked the door behind him, flipped her sign to closed, and then headed to the kitchen washbasin.

Plunging her hands into the water, she scrubbed her fingers with the gentle soap. Then inspected her nails and wiped her hands with a towel. The last thing she needed was someone becoming ill from her baked goods because of dirty work conditions. That would be the ruin of her before she had even started.

A hand landed on the front doorknob of the shop, and she heard someone try to open the door. Her heart thundered, and she tiptoed to the curtain partition that separated the shop from the back room. Trent and Charlie loomed outside the front door, staring through the window. She swallowed hard and waited as they spoke to each other. A minute passed, and then the men disappeared out of sight. She paused to see if they would try the back door of the hut, not that they would succeed in getting it open. She'd spelled the door to the hut as well as the window first thing after her father's attack. No one could see inside the window, and no one except her father or herself could open the door. She wished she could spell the front of the store as well, but if she wanted to continue running a business, she had to let people come inside.

Eloa pressed herself into the wall of the back room and took several deep breaths. She had to keep it together. If they found out the truth about her father, it could mean the end of both of them.

CHAPTER FOUR

A knock awoke Gerall the next morning.

"Come in." He reached for the glasses on his nightstand and looked at his clock. He'd overslept. They'd gone out on patrol again the night before in hopes of finding the missing vampire girl as well as Fendrick. But to no avail.

Jamen popped around the corner of the door. "Morning, sleepyhead."

"Sorry I slept so late."

"Dreaming of the girl who baked those amazing pastries?"

Gerall looked over at Jamen, standing in his doorway.

Jamen threw up his hands. "Hey, if I weren't completely in love with my wife, I'd consider marrying that baker's daughter on the spot. Her baking is extraordinary."

A pair of emerald green eyes flashed into Gerall's mind.

"She is quite beautiful." He cleared his throat, embarrassed to have said that out loud. "I... I mean... She's well... She's..."

Jamen chuckled. "As fun as it is to stand here and listen to you stammer, that isn't why I woke you."

"Has something happened?" Gerall was more than happy to change the subject.

"A messenger arrived from Magistrate Jopin. He's having a birthday celebration for his wife on Friday after the last festivities, and he has invited us all."

Gerall stretched. "That was nice of him."

Jamen nodded. "Problem is, he invited *all* of us, and if we show up without Erik, it will appear strange."

"Why don't just you go then? Tell the magistrate the rest of us were feeling poorly."

"I could." Jamen opened the door wider and leaned against the jamb. "But I have no desire to go."

Gerall nodded. "What about Flint?"

Jamen shook his head.

"I guess I could ask the twins to go. They're the liveliest of us."

"Maybe a little too lively considering the company?"

Gerall's thoughts turned to Eloa. He wondered if she would be there. "Well, you don't want to go, and the twins can't be trusted by themselves."

"Can't be trusted to what?" asked Ian entering the doorframe.

"Who says we can't be trusted?" asked Hass.

Jamen laughed.

"What's going on?" asked Flint.

"It's the party for the Magistrate's wife," said Jamen

"So why can't we go?" asked Hass.

"Because Erik is gone, and Snow is gone, and Kellan is—"

"Gone," Hass whispered.

"There will be a lot of questions," said Flint.

"We're going to the festival this week. Everyone will have seen us already," Gerall said.

"But in a very open place like the festival, I doubt anyone will be too invasive," Flint replied.

"Trust me," said Jamen. "These parties are nothing more than the gossiping of old hens. Nothing good can come of subjecting Scarlet and Zelle to attend."

"But it could also be a good place to find out more about what's going on," Gerall said. "Yesterday at the bakery, two men were hanging around staring at the baker's daughter, Eloa. They stared me down when I came out of her shop, which is something that never would have happened three years ago. I saw her when she'd finished delivering the baked goods to our carriage; she peeked around the corner, scared."

The brothers stood silent for a long moment.

"He's right," Jamen finally said. "We can't wait around for Erik. We said we were going to make our presence known and show our faces more. This is part of it."

Flint nodded. "Then we go."

"But who will we get to watch the babies?" asked Hass.

"We could ask Snow," said Ian.

Jamen nodded. "Snow would love that."

"It's settled then," said Flint. "We all go to the party for the Magistrate's wife."

"Come on," Hass clapped Ian on the shoulder.

"There is food waiting to be eaten at the festival," Ian finished.

"Yeah." Jamen threw Gerall a sly smile. "Gerall's girl sure does know how to bake."

"I wouldn't mention that to your wife," said Flint. "She still thinks her burnt rolls are edible thanks to you."

The brothers groaned.

Eloa pulled her last cartful of baked goods toward the grassy knoll where all the vendors had set up their wares around the maypole and stage. She couldn't help but smile as the minstrels practiced their music. Mr. Blen, the dairyman, had donned the costume of a juggler for the day and currently had four small balls thrown in the air. Three of the local girls tied their shoelaces on the stage, dressed in bright fall colored dresses. Golden flowers and vibrant leaves adorned their hair. Light and laughter filled all of Westfall, and the festival hadn't even started. A portion of the knoll had been sectioned off, and a group of women hid buns and toys and other goodies for the children to find. A band of the townsfolk had apparently gotten together and decided to put on a play. They rushed about with set pieces and costumes all trying to hide their things behind the stage.

Eloa smiled again and set her goods on a long table. The lively colors of her pastries had been designed to catch everyone's eye. She'd stayed up most of the night just making sure every last one of them looked perfect. Since her father's supposed death, she'd barely survived on what the bakery made. And ever since her visits from Trent and Charlie had started, her customer base had dropped drastically. Which was why she'd taken extra steps to make sure that everything not only looked perfect but tasted perfect as well. This was her chance. Even with Lord Gwyn's generous offering, if she couldn't pull the townspeople into her bakery, she'd be no better than a kept woman on his money. And as much as she liked baking, it wasn't what she wanted a man to keep her for.

She set the last cake on the table with care. Three tiers of white cream filled with berry spread and topped with edible flowers. Her masterpiece.

She stepped back to admire her handiwork, promptly bumping into someone. She spun around to find Trent leering at her.

"Hello, sweetie. How are we this fine day?"

Eloa scanned the area. Though everyone busied themselves with their own setup, she doubted Trent would do anything overly threatening with so many witnesses around.

Or so she hoped.

"I'm not your sweetie. Now if you will excuse me, I have to finish." She spun on her heels and moved to her table to arrange the miniature pies.

"It's a beautiful day," said Trent. "Pity your father couldn't be here to see it."

Eloa froze, and a chill raced down her spine.

"He was truly an interesting man, your father. Gutsy, I'll give him that. He never once gave into my protection, and you saw what happened to him. Pity. It all could have been avoided had he just let me protect him."

Eloa spun around. "You stay the hell away from me, or I'll—"

He strode toward her, making her back up into her table. "You'll what, dove? Use magick on me?"

She glanced around at the other vendors. Each glanced at her for a moment before pointedly looking away. Sweat slicked her palms and the urge to pee almost consumed her. They all knew. And none of them were willing to stand up to Trent.

"That's right. I know all about you and your father." He twirled a lock of her long hair. "You can leave your hair down to cover those pointy ears all you want, but I know the truth."

She slapped his hand away.

"I can be nice. I can offer you protection from those who would otherwise see a nice fae girl get thrown out of town. I can save you from the same fate your father suffered. It must have been a terrible way to die. The oven exploding like that." He ran his hand down her arm, his gaze falling on her chest.

Eloa jerked away from his grip. "I'd rather proclaim who I am for everyone to see than have you ever touch me again."

Anger burned so bright inside her she thought she might catch aflame. He reached for her, and without thinking, she grabbed his hand, letting her magick flow down her fingertips, zapping his skin. There was no way she would be treated like a common whore.

His jaw locked, and he gritted his teeth.

"I said. Don't touch me." She released his hand, and he jerked it toward his chest.

Trent spat at her feet, and she fought the gasp that threatened to escape. His disrespect was enough to have her wanting to reduce him to ash right there in front of everyone.

"Are you sure you want to push me? That little caress isn't even close to what I can do." Her fingers twitched.

He massaged his hand and licked his lips before looming closer. "You think I'm scared of you, sweetheart? I've dealt with vampires and werewolves and trust me, they're a hell of a lot tougher than you." He picked up two mini pies and bit into one.

Eloa's jaw clenched tight as did her fists. She fought to keep from unleashing her magick on him.

"I'll be by at the end of the week for the first payment. And if you even think of trying to rat me out to your new beau Gerall Gwyn, I'll slice him from ear-to-ear."

Trent grabbed one last pie and headed toward the stage.

She watched him go, and a wave of nausea washed over her. How many years had this been going on? Trent and Charlie threatening the shopkeepers if they didn't comply? The other townspeople watched Trent walk off and then turned to her with sympathetic gazes. She looked at each of them in turn, swallowing down the bile in her throat. She refused to be seen as weak. Trent had as much as admitted that he'd hurt her father.

Papa! She took off like an arrow across the knoll back toward her house. She raced around the back of the hut and threw her magick at the door, and it flew inward and hit the wall.

She ran toward her father's bed. He wasn't there. Panic swept up her neck.

"Papa? Papa?" She ran into the kitchen, and a wash of relief flooded her as she found him sitting at the table, staring down at a lump of dough. He'd removed the bandages from his arms, and the bright red scarred skin stared back at her. Blood dripped from his hands and smeared the dough.

"Papa." Eloa ran and threw her arms around him.

"I'm useless. Useless. I just wanted to make some bread. I can't even do that anymore."

Eloa lay her hands over her father's cracked and bleeding ones and let her magick flow into him.

"Don't," he protested. "Don't waste your magick. You need it."

"Hush." She wouldn't let him stop her. Not this time. She let magick bathe his hands until the bleeding ceased and the cuts scabbed over. It was as far as she'd ever been able to get him with her magick since she'd never been trained in healing. The sudden drains on her magick left her light-headed. She threw her father's arm over her shoulder.

"Come on," she said. "Let's get you wrapped back up."

"But the Festivus—"

"Can wait."

She needed to find a real healer, or he wasn't going to make it.

Gerall carried baby Marcus while Flint and Zelle followed close behind. With so many people in town, Flint needed extra help steering through the crowd. So, with Zelle by his side and baby Lucia in the pram Jamen had built for Kellan, Flint concentrated on appearing normal. They walked past store after store, trying to make it to the common green where the festivities were being held. People passed them, nodding, bowing, and curtsying. Gerall picked small pieces of horsehair and dirt from his tunic until Scarlet's hand fell lightly on his arm. He looked down at her sweet, smiling face.

"Stop fretting. You look handsome."

Hass came up behind him and squeezed his shoulders. "Don't worry, if she doesn't go for ya, I'll be sure to step in and take your place."

"Yeah, with baking like that I don't even care what she looks like." Ian laughed.

A group squeezed by them, bumping into Flint.

"Stop it," Flint growled after the group had passed. "Gerall has a right not to be bothered by the blathering idiocy of you two dimwits."

Gerall glanced over at Flint. Zelle stopped walking and whispered in Flint's ear.

"Did he just insult us?" asked Hass.

Ian shrugged. "Who knows. I don't listen to half of what he says."

"I think he called us dumb."

"No. He said we were dimwits."

"What does that even mean?"

"I don't know." Ian laughed. "I'm too dimwitted to understand."

Flint rounded on the pair.

"All right," Zelle interjected. "Why don't I take Marcus and Flint and pop into the tailor's shop for a minute. I wanted to get Flint a few new tunics, and Marcus has almost grown out of all his baby clothes."

Gerall laid his sleeping nephew in her arms.

Zelle looked pointedly at the twins. "You all go ahead. We'll meet you in a little bit after the crowd on the street dies down."

Gerall motioned for Hass and Ian to keep moving. The brothers took off with Jamen, Scarlet and the other two babies toward the village fountain.

Zelle, Gerall, and Flint moved to the edge of the sidewalk closest to the buildings. Another group passed by them, nodding and curtsying. Flint stepped into the shade, took off his glasses, and rubbed his eyes. When he opened them again, they were his normal, sightless black color. He laid his large hand on Gerall's shoulder as comfortable as if he'd seen it there.

"I'm sorry I snapped."

Gerall squeezed his big brother's hand. "There is no need to apologize. It's hot, bright and over-crowded. Your overly sensitive hearing must be picking up every nuance."

"I haven't been out among this many people in so long. Even before the loss of my sight..."

"Would you like to go home?" Zelle asked. "I can get Lucia—"

"No." Flint pulled her close and hugged her. "You've

been cooped up in the manor house too long. You deserve some days in the sunshine."

Zelle smiled and laid her head on his chest. "I'm happy just being with you and our children. You know that."

Flint kissed her head.

Gerall's ribcage squeezed. The happiness that Jamen and Flint had found overjoyed him. But it also seemed to emphasize his loneliness.

"I've got him, Gerall," said Zelle. "You go on ahead. We'll catch up after we see the tailor."

Gerall nodded. "If you need anything, just send someone and I'll come right away."

Flint smiled at Gerall. A sight Gerall hadn't seen in so long that it warmed him. "You're a great man, Gerall. Gods above know you're better than me."

"Nah. I just learned from you and Erik."

Flint shook his head. "You're a great man, but a terrible liar. Now, go find your bakery girl."

Gerall inclined his head to Zelle before turning to go.

Butterflies swirled in his stomach, the closer he drew to the green. Only once had he seen Eloa, and yet the prospect of seeing her again made him feel like a ten-year-old boy.

Gerall crested the hill to the grassy knoll, and the swarm of people below made his gut twist. It seemed everyone in Westfall had come out for the beginning of the festivities. Music and dancing drew a crowd toward the stage. Children swarmed around a puppeteer at a small theater. Jugglers and minstrels perused the masses. The maypole wound with little girls in colorful frocks and little boys pitched balls at a stack of wooden pins. There had been years where he'd thought he'd never get a chance to be a part of it again.

He scanned the crowd for Jamen, Hass, and Ian. He found them by the food vendors. Seeing them out there, laughing and having a good time, gave him hope for their future.

When they were young, his mother and father used to be at the heart of the Festivus every year— judging the pie contest— crowning the Festivus queen. Watching the performances and offering flowers to every young girl. A happier time. A simpler time.

Gerall spotted Eloa's table piled high with pastries. People milled about it and pointed at the various items, but Eloa wasn't there. He scanned for her, but couldn't see her anywhere. He headed for the table, weaving through the crowd.

"I don't know," someone said.

"I haven't seen her yet today," said another.

"What do we do?" asked a third. "I'm hungry now."

Gerall ducked behind the table and faced the waiting customers. "I'll help." He glanced around the table and did a quick calculation of everything she'd set out. "Mrs. Pince, what can I get for you this morning?" he asked.

Mrs. Pince blinked several times and looked around the crowd. The woman next to her shrugged.

"I'll take a dozen of the gooseberry muffins please, Lord Gwyn." She gave a slight curtsy.

Gerall laughed. "Please, I'm just Gerall. And as it turns out, today I'm not even a Gwyn, I'm a baker." He spotted a stack of bags and baskets in Eloa's cart. He grabbed a basket and picked out twelve of the muffins and handed the basket to Mrs. Pince.

"That will be two silver pieces, please." He held out his hand for the money.

"Two?" she questioned.

Gerall threw on his best smile. "Trust me. They're worth four for how they taste. If you're dissatisfied, I'll refund you personally."

She pursed her lips and then opened her money satchel and handed him the coins.

"Enjoy." He dropped the coins into a small box on the table. "Who's next?"

The townspeople practically clamored over one another to be next. Gerall helped each in turn, smiled, and thanked them for coming. But every chance he got, he stole glances toward Westfall. He hoped Eloa was all right.

ELOA RACED DOWN TO HER TABLE, ALMOST TRIPPING OVER her gown in the process.

"Sorry," she shouted. "I'm sorry." She pushed through the crowd to find Gerall standing behind her table, giving change to a man as well as a bag of goods.

"Now be sure to come back soon, or it might all be gone."

The man tipped his hat to Eloa, and she fought to catch her breath. Her cheeks flushed with heat as Gerall smiled down at her and pushed his glasses up his nose.

"The festival started thirty minutes ago."

She nodded several times, still trying to still her pounding heart. "I got caught up at home and lost track of time."

"Excuse me," said a woman. "I was next."

Gerall smiled. "Of course. What can I get you?"

"Oh, you needn't do that, Lord Gwyn. I can do it," Eloa replied.

He raised one eyebrow and smirked at her. "Are you saying I can't handle a table of sundries?"

Heat flushed her cheeks hotter. "No. Of course not. That's not—"

He chuckled. "I'm teasing. There are dozens of people waiting. Why don't I help you until the crowd thins a bit?"

Eloa looked around, and sure as day, dozens of people waited to buy her goods. Nervousness lodged in her stomach. "Thank you."

Gerall turned back to a woman, and Eloa watched him until someone else caught her attention and placed an order.

Side by side, they filled baskets, boxes, bags, and pockets with sweets. Minutes turned into an hour and the hour turned into two before there were hardly any pies, cakes or tarts left on her table.

Gerall treated everyone with patience and kindness—even the pushy ones. And he refused to allow anyone to undercut or try to bargain her down. He possessed a quiet strength she envied. When it came to pressure, she froze or panicked. But not him.

He ran his hands through his immaculately styled hair, the color of strong tea, and made it stick up all over. "I think that you have officially won over the entire village and no other baker would dare stand a chance of opening a shop now."

She fought the urge to giggle at his hair. "I do believe that this rush on my bread was due in large part to you, Lord Gwyn."

His eyes widened in surprise. "Me? I did nothing."

"Truly? So, you didn't mention my goods to the magistrate? Or the glassmaker or the stable hand yesterday?"

He gave her a crooked, sheepish grin. "Perhaps I mentioned what an incredible lunch I had. But this. This was all you. I simply helped with advertising."

She looked over the table, gathered up the few remaining broken items, and placed them in a basket.

"I'd expected to be here all day, but with it only being noon and my wares being sold, I'm not sure what to do with myself," she said.

"Surely you planned on enjoying the Festivus. The wishing well cleansing will happen in a couple of minutes. There's entertainment and food, and tonight there will be dancing."

"It's been a long while since I've danced."

"Then, it is decided. You shall stay for the rest of the day and enjoy yourself."

Her gut clenched, and she glanced over her shoulder toward the bakery. She'd rebandaged her father and put him back in bed, but who knew what kind of mischief he could be getting into.

"Is something the matter?"

She looked back to Gerall. "No. Nothing."

"I could help you take your cart back if you'd like."

"No." The words came out too forcefully. "I mean. No, thank you. You've helped quite more than you ought to have." She smiled and pulled a haypence from the box Gerall had kept the money in. "Besides. I owe you a wish."

His thick brows furrowed.

"When I was younger, you did me great kindness. Your father had just cleansed the well for the festivities, and all the children gathered around to make wishes. I had not a haypence to make a wish, so you gave me one."

His head cocked slightly to the side, and then he smiled. "Braids. Your hair was in braids like this." He grabbed her hair and began to lift it.

She jerked away from him reflexively.

His expression fell. "I apologize. I shouldn't have done that."

She tugged on her hair, flattening it to ensure it covered her ears. "No, it's… it's fine. I was just unprepared."

"Anything left?"

Gerall's twin brothers walked up.

"We thought about pushing everyone out of the way and taking it all for ourselves, but we didn't want to upset the regular folks," said the other.

She looked between them, unable to see a single difference in their tanned faces. With blond hair and boyish rugged looks, and wide frames, they appeared so different from Gerall.

"I'm Hass." The first stuck out his hand. "I'm the handsome one." He turned his brother's head and pointed to a missing piece of the other twin's ear.

Eloa shook Hass' hand.

"And I'm Ian. The smart one." He stuck out his hand, and she shook that as well.

"Eloa."

Both brothers looked to Gerall. "Yes, we've heard."

Eloa bit her lip and looked at her toes. Had Gerall mentioned her?

"Have Flint and Zelle arrived?" Gerall asked.

"Yeah. Everyone is waiting on you—"

"For the wishing well ceremony."

Eloa looked between the twins and grinned at how they finished each other's sentences.

Hass leaned in on the table and wiggled his eyebrows. "I could escort you to the ceremony if you'd like."

She snickered, and Gerall took a step closer to her. Hass looked up at Gerall and then straightened again.

"But if Gerall has everything under control then I'll let him escort you."

She looked up at Gerall, who held out his arm to her.

"If you'd care to go, I'd be happy to escort you."

The twins elbowed each other and made strange faces.

"I'd be honored, Lord Gwyn." She went to slip her hand through his arm, but he pulled away.

"I can't take you unless you promise to call me Gerall."

So practical. She loved the fact that he had no need for pretense. "Of course. Sorry. Gerall."

"Wow, if it takes that little to get him not to escort you, I think you should stick with me," said Hass.

"I wouldn't refuse to take you even if you stabbed me in the eye with a fork," said Ian.

She laughed and gave the twins a small curtsy. "I thank you both, but I think Gerall asked first."

"He did?"

"I don't remember it that way."

She slid her hand over Gerall's arm and rested her other hand atop it. "Shall we? I wouldn't want you to keep everyone waiting."

Gerall threw her a crooked grin that made his oak brown eyes crinkle. She dropped her eyes as heat flushed her skin.

Together they walked across the green and back toward the town square where a crowd had gathered for the wishing well cleansing. Eloa refused to look away as the townspeople stared at her with Gerall. But when she met Trent's eye, a chill raced up her spine. He elbowed Charlie, and they both leered at her and tipped their hats.

That problem needed to be handled. Quickly.

CHAPTER FIVE

Eloa stood with the women of Gerall's family while he and his brothers walked to the front of the wishing well for the ceremony.

"We haven't been formally introduced," said Flint's wife. Her beauty was both foreign and unparalleled, with flowing silvery hair and large purple eyes. She stuck out her hand, awkwardly from beneath her sleeping baby. "I'm Rapunzelle. Everyone calls me Zelle, though."

Eloa shook her hand, and the feel of magick flowed through her fingertips. She'd never touched another magickal being before. The sensation of power and familiarity struck a deep chord inside Eloa. Her gaze connected with Zelle's, who gave a quiet, knowing smile, making the hairs on Eloa's neck stand up.

"I… I'm Eloa." She pulled her hand away, unsure of what to say. Was Zelle Fae?

"It's very nice to meet you." Zelle's voice remained low

and soft. "And I'm sure you know Scarlet."

Scarlet pushed the baby pram out of the way and shook Eloa's hand as well. "I think I've seen you about town on occasion." She looked Eloa up and down. "Though I could swear the last time I saw you, you were no more than ten." Her brows furrowed.

Eloa gave a light titter of laughter. "I believe Gerall said the same thing."

Zelle continued to look at her. "Some blossom early and some late."

Scarlet nodded. "I suppose you're right. With everything that's happened in the past couple of years, it all seems a blur."

Zelle nodded. "Indeed."

Flint called for everyone to quiet themselves and then began a speech about the origins of the well and Festivus itself. He wore quite curious red glasses. Beneath them, Eloa had noticed scarring around his eyes. She wondered if some terrible accident had befallen him, like her father.

Father. She looked toward the bakery. She should check on him and make sure he was all right. When she'd left him, he'd told her to enjoy the day, but she'd not been away for more than an hour at a time since his accident. And now with Trent's threats…

"Belle!" Scarlet called.

Eloa turned to find Belle and her daughter Chloe moving through the crowd toward them her belly large and heavy with pregnancy. She wore a beautiful silken gown and Chloe sported satin ribbons in her hair. Eloa had never seen them look so elegant.

"Hello." Belle hugged Scarlet and nodded to Zelle. "I didn't know if we would make it today or not for the ceremony. Dax didn't want me to travel with me so far gone."

"I'm going to have a brother," Chloe announced. She looked at Scarlet's belly. "And you're going to have a girl."

Belle pulled the Chloe close to her side and whispered in her ear. Chloe looked at Eloa and then back to Scarlet.

"I mean, it would be nice if you had a girl."

Scarlet smiled. "That's what we are hoping for."

"Belle, do you know Eloa? She owns the bakery now. Her delicacies are quite delightful," said Zelle.

Belle nodded. "Are you the one who makes the little pies with blueberries and lemon?"

"Guilty."

"Ooohhh mama, I love those ones." Chloe waved at Eloa.

"They're quite a treat," said Belle. "Perhaps you could save one for Chloe today?"

"She's sold out of everything," said Scarlet. "Gerall helped her this morning and before noon, every last item sold."

Chloe's expression fell.

"Are you not going to be here tomorrow?" Eloa asked. "I could set some aside for you."

"I'm afraid not," replied Belle.

"Maybe if Klaus comes into town, he can pick them up for you."

Eloa knew Klaus all too well. On several occasions, he'd come into her shop with little Chloe to buy her a treat of some sort. He'd always given Eloa the shivers. The way he stared at her and the sexual overtones of his words.

"Uh… no." Belle glanced around the ground.

"Belle is married to Prince Dax of the Draaklands," said Zelle. "Klaus is no longer around, I'm afraid."

"Oh… I'm so sorry to hear that."

The women looked at each other awkwardly.

Clapping sounded from all around as Flint finished his speech. Gerall called all the children forward toward the well, and then the brothers proceeded to hand a coin to each child to toss in.

"Flint seems to be doing well," Belle said.

"He struggles," replied Zelle. "Especially in public. But he's getting better each day."

"Uncle Flint's the strong one," said Chloe. "When he fights—"

"Chloe honey." Belle looked around the group nervously and then back at her little girl. "Why don't we go and get you a coin to make a wish with."

Fights?

Belle gave Zelle and Scarlet an apologetic glance and then headed off with Chloe. Eloa looked on as Belle approached Jamen and they embraced before he handed Chloe a coin. Chloe said something that made Jamen laugh, and then the two walked to the well. Hass and Ian smiled and joked with the children, seeing who could throw the kids higher in the air.

"Did you make a wish?" Gerall whispered in her ear, making her jump. She grabbed his arm and a spark of magick jolted from her fingers.

Eloa pulled away quickly. "I... I'm so sorry."

Gerall rubbed his arm where she'd grabbed him. "Sorry. I didn't mean to frighten you."

She gave him a nervous laugh. "You didn't."

He cocked an eyebrow at her.

"Maybe just a little. You're very light on your feet. I didn't even hear you approach."

"I'll have to learn to walk louder in the future." He gave her a large, crooked smile that made her heart dance. "You have a mean grip, you know that?"

She gave a nervous chuckle. "Sorry about that."

"So? Did you?" he asked. "Make a wish?"

"Did you?"

He shook his purse. "All out of coins."

She lifted his palm and pressed a haypence into it.

"How about if we throw it together?" he offered.

"I don't think it works that way."

He placed the coin back in her palm and wrapped his hand around hers, sending goosebumps over her skin.

"It does today."

Eloa allowed his hands to warm hers for a moment. Heavens, she liked the sight of his handsome face. She fought the urge to push his glasses back up his nose.

He offered her his arm, and they headed to the well. The bright white well had been covered in stalks of fluffy wheatburn from the latest harvest. As well as cranberry and tangerine wildflowers.

She held up the coin. "Do you know what you're going to wish for?"

He nodded. "Yes. You?"

She thought for a minute. If she could have anything in the world, what would she want? The answer came to her in a flash. She opened her eyes and nodded.

Together they tossed the coin in the well. She reached up on her tiptoes and leaned over the side, watching the coin disappear into the darkness below, just like she had as a child.

"What did you wish for?" he asked.

She dropped back on her feet and wiped off her hands. "I can't tell you, or it won't come true."

"Is that so?"

She nodded. "Everyone knows that."

Over his shoulder, a figure caught her eyes. Charlie waved at her, sending a chill through her.

"Is something wrong?" Gerall followed her gaze.

"I just… I remembered I need to get my cart back to the shop and start baking for tomorrow."

"Is that man bothering you?"

"No. He's nothing. But I really must go." She needed to check on her father. She'd been gone too long, and she did need to start baking. She couldn't leave it to the last minute, or she'd be too weak to attend the festival tomorrow.

"If he's bothering you, you can tell me."

"Thank you for the lovely day." She turned and pushed through the crowd.

"Eloa? Wait. Let me help you." Gerall caught up with her.

"Lord Gwyn, you've done quite more than I could have asked for today. I can do this on my own." She hitched up her skirt and headed off again, Trent's words echoing in her ears. 'I'll *slit his throat from ear-to-ear.*' The thought of Gerall being hurt made her ears twitch.

"Eloa? Will you come back for the dance tonight?" he called.

She wanted to stop and turn and see his smiling face once more. She wanted to say yes. She imagined herself in his arms while the other young maidens looked on in envy for once. But she couldn't.

She pushed through the townsfolk and headed for the green.

Gerall watched Eloa rush away and then he turned to find the men behind him watching her as well. He refused to allow them to upset her so.

He pushed through the crowd toward them, but as soon as they spotted Gerall, they ducked the other way.

"Gerall?" called Hass.

"Where ya goin'?" asked Ian.

Paying his younger brothers no mind, he continued on his path, following the men who now headed toward the butcher shop. As he came within earshot of them, they turned down an alley.

"Gerall?" Hass caught up to him, and his hand landed on Gerall's shoulder. "What's going on?"

"I need to talk to the two men who just entered that alley." He pressed forward.

"Is there gonna be a fight?" asked Ian. "I could use a good fight."

Gerall crossed the dirt road to the butcher shop and looked down the alleyway. The men had disappeared.

"Slow down," said Hass.

"Let us help," said Ian.

Gerall stared down the alleyway. The hairs on his neck prickled as they had before. Something wasn't right. The way they made Eloa uneasy made him want to rip their arms off and beat them to death. A gentle, sweet creature such as her didn't deserve to be hassled by two thugs.

Jamen and Erik had learned the year previous that someone in Westfall had determined to put an end to their rule of the countryside. But those at the top of the list had to have bottom feeders doing their bidding. And Gerall had a good idea those two men might be the key to finding out what was going on in Westfall.

"You gonna tell us what's going on?" Hass finally asked.

"I don't know," Gerall admitted. He shook his head and turned from the alley. "They've been watching Eloa and her shop. Every time she sees them, she gets nervous."

"Are you sure that's not just you being over-protective?" asked Hass.

Gerall pushed up his glasses and gave his brother a pointed look. "No. It isn't me just trying to protect her. Something is unsavory about them."

"Well, there's nothing we can do about it right now," said Ian.

"Come on." Hass clapped Gerall on the shoulder. "Let's head back to the festival. Ian and I will be sure to keep an eye out for them."

"And if we see them," said Ian. "We'll be sure to invite

them to tea."

"Maybe we could knock them out by throwing Scarlet's biscuits at them." Hass laughed.

"At least they'd be good for something."

Gerall glanced down the alleyway again ignoring his brothers' banter. "The last thing we need in Westfall is ruffians running roughshod over the townsfolk. It's very well possible that in our absence, others have taken it into their hands to try and position themselves as the authorities in town."

Hass cracked his knuckles. "Well if that's true, then we'll just have to make sure they're knocked down a peg."

Gerall shook his head. "No. Nothing gets rough unless we have to. We've been out of touch for too long. The last thing we want is everyone thinking we're trying to become dictators."

"See. That's why I love you, big brother," said Ian. "You're always thinking with your head and not your fists."

Gerall smiled, and as he turned toward the festivities, he spotted Eloa pulling her cart up toward her bakery. He stepped in her direction, but then stopped. A woman as strong as she wouldn't appreciate been viewed as weak. He needed to wait. To give her space. They had time.

Eloa made dozens of goods over the rest of the afternoon and evening, using up almost all of her supplies. She'd need to go to the grocer to stock up if she wanted any chance of continuing.

She stared at the cakes, pies, pastries and other items she'd made. Simple ingredients no better than anyone else's. The difference between her goods and theirs was simple. She was half-fae.

She made sure to lock the front door and close the curtains to the back room before rolling up her sleeves and waving her hands over the sundries. Magick sprinkled onto the food, turning everything various bright shades of sungold and cherry. Deep cream for vanilla. Luscious brown for cinnamon and nutmeg. Purple, blue, green, and more depending on flavor. The items puffed even more abundant than they otherwise would have been. The rough spots or ill-formed shapes smoothed out to perfection to tantalize any taste bud.

When she'd finished, she leaned against the counter and sucked in a deep breath. The pull on her magick tired her quicker than she'd expected, but she had used it much that day. A gnawing, guilty sensation churned in her gut. Was it cheating to use magick to make money?

"Other people use their talents and gifts to make their wares, why should I be any different?"

"Because it can get you banished or worse, imprisoned."

She spun to find her father leaning on the counter. "Papa, you should be resting."

"No. I should be leaving."

"Nonsense. We've talked about this. You aren't going anywhere." She picked up a plate and set several items on it and then crossed to him. "Come on. Let's get you fed."

He nodded sadly, and she helped him to the small wooden table in the middle of their hut.

"I know that not being able to work is hard for you Papa, but we'll figure this out. We'll get you healed and find out who did this to you, and—"

He stared at his bandaged hands. "I know who did this." His voice came out so low she almost thought she'd heard him wrong.

She set the food on the table. "You know who did this?"

He nodded.

"Why didn't you tell me? Who did this? I'll see that they pay."

He looked up at her with a sad, fearful expression. "It will only bring more attention to you. They think I'm dead and that's all that matters."

She studied him for a minute. "It was Trent and Charlie, wasn't it?"

He didn't deny it. "Leave it alone, child."

"Trent came by my table today. He told me he knew about you and me. He offered to keep quiet if I…" She couldn't finish the sentence. "He said he'd be by the end of the week to collect a gold piece."

"A gold piece?" said her father.

"How much did they try to get from you?" she asked.

Her father's cheeks deepened.

"I know they used to shake you down. And from the looks of all the other shopkeepers today, we aren't the only ones. I wouldn't be surprised if everyone has been paying them." A memory of Trent's words floated through her mind. "They threatened to tell the Magistrate about me. Surely someone would have gone to either him or the

Gwyns if only Trent and Charlie were involved with the blackmail."

"Which means they aren't afraid," said her father. "They're protected."

"Mayhaps they are cutting the magistrate in for a piece of what they take."

Her father stared off for several minutes. "Mayhaps. But I doubt that man could be behind all of this. He doesn't have the brains." He looked at her. "You should tell your new friend, Gerall."

Eloa shook her head vehemently. "They threatened to kill him. I would see no harm done to him because of my plight."

"But it isn't just your plight. If what you say is true, then everyone in Westfall may be affected."

She licked her lips.

"You should tell him."

If she told Gerall, then she'd have to tell him what Trent and Charlie had over her as well and then she'd be banished. She closed her eyes and blew out a deep breath. What were she and Gerall playing? Yes, she'd had a girlhood crush on him for years, but once he found out she was half-fae, it would all be over. His attention and looking after her. His sweet smiles and gentle manner. For years she'd dreamed of no one but him, and now that he'd finally noticed her, she had to let him go because of her heritage. Or maybe not… She remembered Flint's wife, Zelle.

"Father. I might know someone I can turn to."

"Who?"

"Rapunzelle Gwyn. I think she's fae."

CHAPTER SIX

Eloa hadn't shown up to the dance the night before. And silly as it sounded, Gerall had woken up with the same disappointed feeling he'd gone to bed with. Gerall barely knew the girl and yet, he wanted to know her, and so her absence had affected him more than he'd expected it to.

He'd enjoyed both the music and the company of his brothers, Hass and Ian. At one point, they'd dragged him out onto the dance square and forced him to dance with a pretty maiden, but all Gerall could see of the girl was that she wasn't Eloa. Afraid of leaving his riotous brothers alone, he'd waited until they'd worn themselves out with dancing and mead before getting them back on their horses and listening to their terrible singing the whole way home. Watching them revel in the celebration had lifted his spirits. The two never seemed to let anything weigh them down. He envied that about them.

The following morning, Gerall tended to several animals owned by their farmer tenants. He didn't want to be an animal doctor, but it was a place to start until he felt comfortable working with humans.

Months back, Erik had said that since their hunter services were hardly needed, he should look to the future like Flint and Jamen. And even though he sometimes took over duties for Erik temporarily, Gerall wasn't going to be Lord of Gwyn Manor. Erik and Flint had never made him feel lesser than they were, but the Lordship moved from father to eldest son, and unless something happened to both his older brothers, he wouldn't be Lord of the Manor. And Gerall didn't mind that at all. He preferred a simpler life at home with his family, studying and helping people more than he ever would meetings and taxes and being forced to attend engagements with people he had no desire to spend time with.

By lunchtime, he dragged himself back to the manor house and opened the solar door to find his brothers playing cards. The smell of cooking meat wafted out of the kitchen.

"Good! You're back. Now you can help us keep Jamen from taking all of our money," said Flint, throwing his cards onto the table.

"It's not my fault I'm good at cards, and you all show your hand on your faces." Jamen smiled.

"I still think you cheat," said Hass.

"Yeah," said Ian. "No one's that good."

"You've been saying that since you were twelve, Hass."

"There's chicken if you want some." Flint motioned toward the kitchen.

Gerall glanced through the open doorway. A plate and fork lay on the counter next to a loaf of Eloa's bread. His thoughts turned to Eloa and seeing her again.

"I thought we were going into town today for the festival," he said.

His brothers chuckled.

"The babies are napping," said Jamen. "We'll go when they awaken."

Gerall crossed to the bread and cut a piece. "Do we need to get a present for the Magistrate's wife? I could go ahead and find one."

"Why?" Jamen's eyebrows wiggled. "You want to go see your bakery girl?"

Gerall flushed. "I just want to make sure we do the right thing."

"Then why are you so red in the face?" asked Ian.

"Because it's warm in here," Gerall retorted.

"Not because she makes your blood rise?" asked Hass.

"Don't talk about her like that!"

His brothers burst out laughing. Gerall scowled and turned his back on them once more. Why had he become so attached to her in the last two days? He hadn't spent more than a few hours with her in total and yet he couldn't get her sweet face out of his thoughts.

"Come on, Gerall. We're just fooling with you. You've never mentioned a girl before," said Jamen.

"That's not true. I used to talk about Gertrude."

"Gertrude was your tutor." Flint snorted.

"Still a girl." Gerall bit into his bread. "And if I

remember correctly, Erik was found in the pantry with Gertrude with his hands somewhere they didn't belong."

"What?" asked Hass and Ian together.

"How come we didn't know this?" asked Jamen.

Quick as that, the topic changed from Eloa to Gertrude, and then to several other servants, and wenches, that had been the conquests of one or more of his brothers. Gerall fetched some food and sat at the table listening to his brothers regale each other with stories of their youthful conquests, just like times past.

He himself had never made love to a woman before. Not that his brothers knew that. He'd done a lot of exploring with them, but never the actual act. Between all of the novels he'd read as well as the medical tomes about the female anatomy, he'd done a lot of experimenting to find out exactly what brought a woman to the heights of arousal, and so each one that his brothers had sent his way had left his company so completely satisfied that he wondered if they even realized he hadn't had sex with them.

His mother had raised them with the understanding that lovemaking was both intimate and sacred. His brothers hadn't learned the lesson well, but he had. So he'd saved himself until he found the right one. He felt it only fair to his would-be wife but also to any of the other women out there.

"Then it's settled," said Flint.

Gerall looked up from his plate. "Sorry, what?"

They laughed again, and Flint shook his head. He removed his red glasses and rubbed his eyes. "Go to town.

Figure out a present for the Magistrate's wife. And see your baker girl while you're at it. Zelle says Eloa's special."

"What does that mean?" asked Hass.

Flint shrugged. "All Zelle would say is that she likes the girl."

"Who doesn't?" asked Ian. "With baking like that and those eyes—"

Gerall tipped his plate sideways, spilling his chicken bones and potatoes in Ian's lap. Ian jumped to his feet as Hass burst out laughing.

Gerall got up from the table and cleared his plate. "Sorry about that."

Ian threw a piece of potato at Hass who caught it in his teeth.

"I'm sure you are," Ian replied.

Gerall set his plate in the washbasin. The thought of seeing Eloa again made him smile. And strangely, so did his brothers' jibes about her.

Gerall headed to the stable, and the stableman emerged. *Armie!* His name was Armie.

"Hello, Armie," Gerall said.

Armie beamed. "Hello Lord Gwyn. It's nice to see you again."

"And you. Have you been to the festival today?"

"For an hour or so. They are having the children's surprise hunt in a few hours. And the Magistrate opened up his flower garden for viewing. Some of the most beautiful fall blooms ever. His wife sure does know how to tend to plants."

"I can't wait to see them."

Armie looked at Gerall and opened his mouth, but then licked his lips.

"You have something to say?" Gerall asked.

"I just… I wanted to say that I'm delighted your sister found someone nice to marry. The last time I saw her, I'm afraid I failed her."

Gerall's eyebrows scrunched together. "Failed her?"

Armie looked away. "She came in as Klaus, and a couple of his friends roughed me up, due to a debt. She stood up to them. I… I should have never let her do that for me. She could have gotten hurt. Anyway, after that, I had a few strange things happen, and I barely escaped alive from a pond that tried to suck me through a hole."

"A pond?"

"Klaus took a bunch of us there and told us to swim out to the middle. We did, and then there was a flash of light. Everyone else got sucked into some hole, but I grabbed on to a bar or something at the bottom of the pond and held my breath until the light stopped. Then I waited until I couldn't hold my breath anymore and swam for the surface."

"Armie, why didn't you tell anyone this before?"

He shrugged. "Who would have believed me?"

If Gerall himself hadn't gone through that pond and down to the mirror to get to Tanah Darah, he wouldn't have believed Armie either.

"The Magistrate investigated the missing people, but we haven't seen any of them since."

Nor would they.

Armie scratched the back of his neck. "I suppose what I'm trying to tell you is that I know you and your family are the reason I am alive. And I owe you a life debt. I'm not much, but if you ever need anything. Anything at all. Please call on me. I'll not fail you again."

His sincerity struck Gerall hard. "Thank you, Armie." He stuck out his hand, and Armie stared at it a minute before smiling and shaking. "I need to get going, but thank you for telling me. It seems that we have failed you as well as the people of Westfall in the past few years. But that is a situation we plan on remedying post haste."

Armie beamed. "It's good to see you all back in Westfall again. I'll be sure to take good care of Dugger for you."

"I don't doubt that." Gerall patted his horse's flank and then walked out of the stable and down the street, past the closed shops. Having someone in debt to them might come in handy one day.

Gerall stopped and looked out over the green bustling with more people than the previous day. He spotted Eloa's cart in the same spot it had been the day before. She shoved several empty baskets into her cart and shook out a couple of pieces of fabric.

Gerall smiled at the sight of her and headed toward where she already began packing up. "Seems I'm a bit late."

Eloa looked up from her basket and smiled, crinkling the corners of her eyes that shined like expertly cut jewels. "I'm afraid so."

Did they sparkle for him? Or just because of the sunlight?

"Another good day then?" he asked.

"Better than yesterday. I sold out within an hour."

"I'm happy for you. But sad for me."

They stared at each other for a moment. Her thick, brown hair curled over her cheek. He wished he could push it from her face, but she gave a small, breathy laugh and pushed it away herself.

"If you want, I could run back to the bakery and fetch you something. It won't take but a minute."

"You don't have to do that. It's quite all right."

"I don't mind. I need to stretch my legs and take my cart up anyway."

"How about I help you pack and pull your cart and then you can give me a loaf of bread and some butter."

She looked him up and down. "I don't think you're particularly dressed for pulling a cart?"

He chuckled. "Would you believe that not too long ago I tromped through an unmucked barn?"

"Truly?" Skepticism rooted on her lovely face.

"One of our farmers has a mare about to give birth. I've been tending to her."

"I didn't know you did that."

"I smell perfectly civilized if that is your worry." He stepped closer to her. "You can see for yourself if you'd like."

She took a step away. "You don't need to. I believe you if you said you did it."

He loved that she had no pretense about her. That what he saw was what he got with her. That she didn't fawn over him in hopes that he would bring her status, or wealth or privilege. Many times girls had flirted with him only to find out he was third in line for the Lordship and then suddenly become conveniently busy with other things in their lives. Not that he minded. He'd never wanted even one of them.

"Letting me help you is the only way I'll allow you to feed me," he said.

She pressed her lips together and inclined her head. "Fair enough."

He rounded the table and helped her load her baskets and plates into her cart. At one point, he looked down and caught her sniffing his arm. He stifled a laugh and continued to load her things. Then he grabbed the handles and pulled the cart across through the crowd. People stopped to watch as they passed, but Gerall smiled and nodded.

"This doesn't feel right," she said. "I'm used to doing things for myself. And people are staring."

"But I was raised to be a gentleman. You may be independent, but you're still a lady and deserve to be treated as such."

She peeked up at him from behind thick dark lashes and gave him half a smile. "Did your sister teach you that?"

He gripped the wagon tighter and headed toward the street.

"No. My mother. But Snow never let me forget it."

Her expression sobered. "I'm sorry for all of your losses of late. First, your mother, then your father and your brother. So much sadness."

Silence stretched between them for a minute.

"I was always jealous of your sister growing up."

"Snow? Why?"

She shrugged. "Because she was fortunate to have all of you brothers and a mother and father. My mother died when I was little, and my father has been a great comfort to me, but I always wanted a big family. Siblings to play with and talk to."

He wondered if she would still be jealous if she knew the truth about his family. His beloved sister was now a vampire. He and his brothers hunted vampires. Flint was blind due to a magician's spell and married to a daemon. Their closest friends were werewolves, vampires, and fae. Yes, his family was more than colorful. And he doubted many in Westfall would accept them because of it.

"We have been blessed, that's for sure," he said. "But if you talked to Snow, you'd know it hasn't always been roses for her. Seven brothers chasing off every suitor. Seven to be bossed around by. Seven times more dirty, stinky laundry. And seven more reasons to have to worry and try to keep out of trouble."

"I'm sure you weren't all that bad."

"Maybe not. But Snow would tell you there were many days she wished that she were an only child."

They reached the door to Eloa's bakery.

"Would you like me to pull this around back for you?"

"No." The word came out forcefully, and she laid her hand on his arm. "I mean. Going to the front will be fine. I'll need to unload all the baskets anyway."

He remembered how she'd rushed out of the back room the first time he'd come into the shop a few days before. A trickle of curiosity sprinkled over him.

"Do you need to bake again today?" he asked.

She nodded. "The crowds are getting bigger and bigger when I set up."

A loud bell rung and Gerall looked over his shoulder to see people streaming out of the church.

The town clock read only twelve-thirty, and it was a weekday.

"That's odd."

"Isn't it?" she said. "Just a few months ago, Father Ohana couldn't get ten people in that church on Sundays. Now he has a few dozen that show up almost daily."

Father Ohana stood outside the faded white building and shook hands with everyone who exited.

"But the church has been little more than limping along for the last fifty years."

"I know. But word is a month, or so ago he performed a miracle."

Gerall's head whipped her direction. "A miracle? What kind of miracle?"

She shook her head. "Something about curing a deaf man, I think."

He chuckled. "Surely, you jest?"

"I don't believe it either, but there it is. At least that's what the people are saying. Some say he's been healing others as well, but they won't explain."

A pit lodged in Gerall's stomach, and he turned back to see Father Ohana head back into the church. If the priest was healing people, it wasn't by divine intervention.

CHAPTER SEVEN

Eloa wanted to tell Gerall that she suspected magick, but she didn't want to draw attention to her own secrets.

"I owe you some bread and butter." She pulled out her keys and unlocked the front door of the shop. "What kind of bread would you like?" she asked loud enough for her father to hear in the back. "We have butter bread, herb bread, brown bread, and cinnamon."

The hairs on Eloa's neck prickled and she jumped. Gerall snuck up right behind her.

"Herb would be wonderful," he said in her ear. "But why are you yelling?"

The nearness of his body made her skin flush with heat as she stared up into his face. He stood a good foot taller than she did, and his arms upon closer inspection were fuller than she'd realized. Her gaze traveled to his lips, and for a moment, she wondered what they'd feel like pressed against hers.

She blinked several times, removing the desire that had taken root and gave a nervous smile. "Was I yelling? I'm sorry. Must be because I got used to having to speak over the noise all morning. If you want to sit at the counter, I'll be just a minute."

His eyes searched her face. She rubbed her forehead, trying to collect her thoughts. *The ovens!*

"I need to light the ovens."

"Can I get you some wood?"

She started for the backroom. "No, thank you. I have plenty stockpiled. Just have a seat."

He inclined his head and pushed his glasses up his nose before walking to the counter to sit. What was wrong with her?

Eloa took a deep breath, trying to calm herself, and then walked through the curtain before loading wood into the ovens and flicking her fingers to light them. She glanced over her shoulder, but the curtain remained shut. *Reckless.* Too reckless. But… he had to know his sister-in-law held magick, didn't he?

"Eloa?" Her father stood in the doorway.

She shook her head and motioned for him to go back.

"Are you sure you don't need help?" Gerall called.

Eloa rushed over and grabbed a loaf of bread from the shelf and cut several thick slices.

"I'll be but a moment." She plated the bread and then slathered butter on the pieces and grabbed a jar of preserves.

Her father watched her, and she shooed him away.

Eloa waited until he moved out of sight before walking back out front. She plastered a smile on her face and set the plate and preserves in front of Gerall.

He cocked his head to the side, and his eyes narrowed on her.

"What?" She crossed her arms over her chest.

"That smile. I'd swear you were trying to hide something with it."

She gave a titter of nervous laughter. "I don't know what you mean."

His eyebrows lifted. "I'm sure you do, but I won't pry."

She wiped her hands on the front of her dress. "Would you like something to drink? Water? Wine? Mead?"

"Water would be just fine, thank you."

She nodded and headed to the back to fetch a pitcher and a cup. By the time she returned, he'd finished two of the three pieces of bread.

"Can I get you more?"

He shook his head. "No. Thank you, I should stop." He stared at her for a moment before breaking off a small section of the last piece of bread and popping it in his mouth. "Tell me something about you, Eloa."

"What do you want to know?"

"Surprise me."

She thought for a moment. What could she tell him that would be interesting? Or, that wouldn't give too much away? She'd spent her entire life in the building she now stood in. She'd never seen anything past the edge of the village. Her days had been filled with learning and baking. Her nights with dreams of getting away. That was all she'd had for the last forty-five years.

"I didn't mean to strain you." He chuckled. "May I ask you some questions?"

She fought the urge to fidget. "All right."

"How old are you really?"

She swallowed. "Older than you think, but not so old as to be considered a matron."

He smiled broadly, tugging her own mouth into a smile.

"A very polite way of telling me that a lady never tells her age, I suppose. All right." He nodded, contemplating. "What's your favorite color?"

"Yellow. But I cannot wear it, unfortunately. It doesn't favor me well."

"Interesting. So, what about flowers? Do you like sungolds?"

"Very much. Though I don't see them here in town often."

"And what about your life? Did you always want to be a baker?"

"I… I enjoy baking. I enjoy making something that people appreciate. And I'm good at it."

"That you are and better than almost anyone, but is it what you want to do? When you were little, what did you dream of becoming when you grew up?"

"A performer, maybe."

He let out a crack of laughter, but it didn't come out as scoffing or jeering. She doubted a kind man like Gerall could ever make fun of someone.

"What kind of performer? An actress?"

She shrugged. "I could never decide. I know how to juggle, so I thought of doing that for a while. I taught myself how to do flips and tricks too. I can walk on my hands and bend my body backward. For a while, I thought about joining a touring troop."

"Why didn't you?"

She brushed her hair back and patted it down over her ears. "I don't know. It was a silly girl's fantasy. I just always thought I would be a baker. My parents were bakers. My mother's parents were bakers. I've never really known anything else, to be honest. What about you? What do you want to be now that you're grown? Or does being a Lord fulfill you?"

"Being a Lord is just a title. It's not who I am. I've always enjoyed medicine and science."

"Truly?"

He nodded. "I've studied as much as I'm able. Snow and my mother used to teach me about herbs. I've gotten my hands on just about every book on the subject I could find. And I have… several friends who are healers that have taught me things here and there as well."

"Do you practice medicine?"

"I've been helping some of our tenant farms with their animals for now."

"That's amazing," she said. "Do you know much about burns?"

He ate another piece of his bread. "Burns? Some. Why? Have you burned yourself?"

"No. I just… well yes. I mean, yes. I have burned myself in the past. Not now. I anticipate that in the future, I most likely will again, and it would be nice to know how to treat them." She kicked herself mentally. Could she be any more awkward? She needed to tread more carefully as not to arouse his suspicion.

"Depending on how extensive they are, you can use several things to help heal a burn. Fernblend works well, but you must keep it moist. Calendula and comfrey can help both heal and soothe."

"What about a bad burn. Say, if the oven exploded or the bakery caught on fire?"

Their eyes connected, and an expression of sadness overtook him. "Like your father?"

She dropped her gaze to her hands. She didn't want to alert him to her father's situation but anything Gerall might be able to do to help him heal, she had to do.

"Yes. Like what happened to my father."

He reached out and squeezed her hand. "I'm sorry. I didn't mean to upset you."

She let the feel of his warm hand wrap around hers settle inside her. Her heart galloped so hard she feared it might give out.

"You didn't," she croaked. She cleared her throat. "I asked the question and should have known you're smart enough to know exactly what I meant by it."

Silence hung between them for a moment.

He pulled his hand away and sat back on the stool. "To answer your question. For extreme burn cases, I would recommend a true healer. A magickal healer."

"But there aren't any of those around here."

His lips clamped down in a tight line. "No. No, there

aren't."

Thwarted again. Maybe if she traveled to Ville DeFee, she could find someone and convince them to help her.

"Do you need to get started baking?" he asked.

She looked up at the clock. "Oh, bother. It's three. I'll not get done before midnight."

"I can help," he offered.

"No. Please, you don't need to."

"I want to." He licked his lips as if deciding something. "I like spending time with you, Eloa. So, don't think of it as me helping you as much as it is me being selfish and trying to find anything that will allow me to talk to you a while longer."

She couldn't help but smile as her cheeks heated. "Well, when you put it that way, how can I say no?"

"You can't." He stood from his chair. "I will warn you though, I know nothing of baking, but I follow directions well."

"Well, the first thing we need to do is go pick up my supplies. I ran out last night."

Gerall nodded. "Let's do that."

They walked to the local shop, and Gerall helped her with her fifty-pound bag of flour, a thirty-pound bag of sugar and various other items. On their way back she once again noticed how nicely filled out he'd become in the last few years.

Back in the shop, they spent the next hour measuring and stirring and preparing dough for five different types of baked goods. It took longer not using magick, but she enjoyed the time they spent together talking. He told her what it had been like, growing up with so many siblings; at the manor house with room to run, and play, and explore. And she told him what it had been like growing up an only child in a one-room house with only books and dolls to entertain herself with. By the end of it, he'd convinced her that a large family was what she wanted.

"So, what do we do now?" he asked.

She brushed the flour from her hands and pushed a stray hair from her eyes. "Now, we wait. It won't take them too long to rise because the ovens keep it so warm in here. Maybe an hour or so."

"And what do you propose we do for an hour?"

"I don't know." In honesty, she didn't care as long as she did it with Gerall.

"Here." He leaned in close. "You have something on your cheek." He punctuated the word cheek by wiping a dollop of leftover dough on her face.

She dropped her jaw in mock surprise. "Why Gerall Gwyn. Did you just put dough on my face?"

His eyebrows rose in feigned innocence. "Nope. Not me."

She leaned back against the counter and grabbed a handful of flour. "And I thought you were a gentleman." She threw the flour at him and then covered her mouth and giggled. The meal caked his glasses, nose, mouth, and even made it into his hair.

He blew out, and a puff of flour floated in the air as he removed his glasses and opened his eyes. They appeared even deeper brown surrounded by all the white.

"Yes. I believe I did say I was a gentleman." He blew on his glasses and then wiped them on the sleeve of his cream tunic. "I suppose that was a lie though because a gentleman would never do this."

Faster than she could imagine he slipped his glasses back on, grabbed a handful of flour and threw it back at her. Before she could react, they broke into an all-out flour fight.

They chased each other through the backroom lobbing flour and bits of dough onto every surface. It flew through the air and coated everything from the ovens to the tables to the wall sconces. He chased her around the central workbench until finally he caught up with her and grabbed her around the waist. In his other hand, he held a giant pile of flour.

"You wouldn't," she said.

He weighed the flour in his hand and looked at it.

Flour dusted his hair, and she wanted nothing more than to run her fingers through his waves and clear it away.

"I might," he said. "Or–"

"Or?"

"I could spare you. If you will be so kind as to accompany me to see the Magistrate's flower garden."

His eyes held a playful glint.

She wanted to. Gods above she wanted to go anywhere he asked, but she had to finish baking. "But the dough…"

"Forty-five minutes. That's all. We'll go. We'll see the flowers and come back in time to put everything in the ovens."

"But how? We're covered in flour."

He dropped the handful of flour and pulled her close.

His arm felt heavy and right wrapped around her waist.

"We can wash up in your hut and be out of here in five minutes."

Her hut? "No. I… I mean… It's quite messy right now. I've been so busy I haven't cleaned it in nearly a week."

His gaze slid to the door that separated her hut from the bakery. When he looked back at her, a sly smile crept across his face.

"Fair enough. Then no flower garden I suppose. But I'm not quite sure how I'll explain all this to my brothers. They're to be arriving soon. If they haven't already."

"Well… we could brush each other off," she offered.

His left eyebrow arched. "All right. You can go first." He released her from his grip and stood perfectly still.

Her heart pounded. He'd given her permission to touch him. She licked her lips and reached up slowly and removed his glasses. She set them on the table, and he closed his eyes as she brushed her fingers across his cheeks. Her fingers trembled as she ran them down his throat and across his chest to his broad shoulders.

She flicked the flour from his clothes and then back up, pinching a spot on his earlobe. His hands fell heavily on her hips, and he pulled her closer to him. Her heartbeat thrummed against her ribcage. She stared into his passive face as she raked her fingers through his thick brown waves. His soft hair rolled through her fingers and sent goosebumps swimming up her arms.

He bowed his head and opened his eyes. Her arms fell around his neck, and neither of them spoke. Her stomach clenched with anxiety.

"My turn." His voice came out in a low, husky whisper.

He brushed the flour from her arms and bodice in slow, circular motions. His palms caressed across her breasts, and she held back a moan of pleasure. Nervousness mixed with desire. She'd never had a man touch her that way before. She'd never had a man touch her in any way.

Up over her throat, his fingers traced, to her jawline. His eyes never left hers, and the heat between them rivaled that of the surrounding ovens.

He ran his thumb across her jaw and up her cheeks. His head dipped lower until his lips were less than ten inches from hers. He cupped her face and then worked his fingers through her hair and up toward her ears.

She wanted nothing more than to feel his lips on hers. He rolled her earlobes through his fingers and then slid them up toward—

Eloa jerked back. The heat between then washed away like a bucket of ice water had been thrown on them. Her ears. If he touched them at the top, he'd know the truth. That she wasn't human.

"I'm sorry," she said. "My ears are… very sensitive is all." It wasn't a total lie.

He inclined his head. "No. It's I that am sorry."

"It's perfectly fine. No harm done."

"Yes," he mused.

She was losing him; she could see it in his expression.

"Do you still want to go to the garden?" she asked.

"Do you?" He picked up his glasses and put them back on.

"Absolutely."

He gave her a soft smile. "Wonderful. Then let us go before our time runs out."

He held out his arm to her, and she linked hers with it. She needed to be careful. Very, very careful.

"THAT COULD BE A PROBLEM," MAGISTRATE JOPIN whispered to the man standing next to him. His gaze followed Gerall and Eloa as they moved about his garden enjoying various flowers and smelling them.

"Not so. In the end, that could play well into our hands if she is indeed what you think she is."

"Oh, she's half-fae all right. See how she hides her ears?"

The man shrugged. "Maybe that's just the way she likes to wear her hair."

"It isn't. I know it." The Magistrate continued to watch as his wife walked up and shook hands with them both. Eloa pointed to a deep crimson cluster of flowers. His wife nodded and smiled.

"How are our guests doing?"

The Magistrate's gaze slid to his friend. "The vampire is a problem."

"She's been a problem since we took her. But since our plan for her didn't roll out the way we had hoped, perhaps it's time we let her go from her terrible existence."

The Magistrate clenched his fists. "Stupid Jamen Gwyn. If he'd not figured out she didn't kill the doctor and his wife, this would all be going much smoother."

"Kill the vampire. We still have the werewolf."

"That is an unstable man if I've ever seen one. All he's done is cry for his wife. The men can't even get near him to give him food."

"Good. The worse off he is, the better this will play out."

The Magistrate cleared his throat. "Are people going to get hurt?"

"Most likely." The man waved at the Magistrate's wife. "You're not thinking of backing out, are you?"

"Of course not."

"This is for the good of Westfall that we do these things. The Gwyns have been in power too long. As soon as people begin to feel the weight of the true threats to Westfall and how the Gwyns aren't able to protect them, they'll turn to you for leadership. And that's when you and your men will step in and seize control."

The Magistrate nodded. Westfall would be his. He deserved it. He'd been the one to care for it and take care of it while the Gwyns shut themselves in their house for the past three years. Their time had passed. His turn to rule had finally arrived.

"When should we release the werewolf?" he asked.

The man clapped him on the shoulder. "You let me take care of that." He straightened his tunic and walked down the garden path in the opposite direction.

The Magistrate kept his eyes fixed on Gerall Gwyn. He was going to enjoy watching the Gwyns crawl back into their manor and rot.

CHAPTER EIGHT

Eloa dragged herself into bed that night, exhausted. Between spending her entire day with Gerall and then having to use her magick to finish off her wares, she could barely keep her eyes open when her head hit the pillow at ten o'clock. Her father's soft snores kept her company as her mind replayed her moments with Gerall. The baking and the flour fight. His hand on her hip, his arm about her waist, his lips so close to hers. He would have kissed her. She knew he would have, but she hadn't wanted him to find out what she was. Not when they were just getting to know each other.

In her heart, she was sure he wouldn't care. But what if he did? What if he didn't know about Zelle? Or what if he cared, though his brothers didn't seem to? She'd have to take the risk and tell him at some point but… not yet. For now, her secret needed to stay safe— both about her, as well as her father.

She smiled as she thought of Gerall again as she drifted off to sleep. Not many men of his status would help her with something as menial as baking bread.

Gerall pulled his horse to a stop outside the family stable and jumped to the ground. The twins followed suit. He opened the door and stepped inside, leading Duggar behind him. He passed the first stall and stopped. *Vrulian.*

The steed popped his head out to greet them.

"Looks like Erik's back," said Hass.

"Guess he still hasn't found the girl," Ian replied.

The three continued onward, then cleaned and brushed down their horses before heading into the manor house.

Erik sat at the solar table with Flint and Jamen. Various items from Eloa's shop sat on the table.

"Anything?" Gerall asked.

Erik shook his head. "Nothing good. The parents of the missing girl are causing trouble. Alluding to the fact that we aren't capable of finding the girl and that they should form their own search party."

"That's the last thing we need. Vampires down here hunting for her."

"Exactly," said Erik. "From what I saw, my guess is that we have less than a week to find the girl before all hell breaks loose and Sage has to take firm action against the parents."

"He won't let them come down here," said Gerall.

"No, he won't, but it might mean an all-out rebellion if

he doesn't. It's a sticky situation, to say the least." Erik sat silent for a minute staring at the table. "And what about you? Anything new?"

Hass and Ian shook their heads.

"It may not be anything, but Father Ohana has apparently been performing miracles. The church had about thirty people in it today for a noon service," said Gerall.

"A miracle?" Flint snorted. "That'll be the day."

"I agree," said Erik. "It's nothing for us to be concerned with anyway. If the people want to believe such nonsense, let them. It does us no good to try and dispute it. We have other problems. We need to figure out where the vampire girl and the werewolf Fendrick are."

Erik stood. "Hass, Ian, you come with me. We'll go out and see if we can find anything tonight. We'll head as far south as Ville DeFee."

"Don't you think you might do better if you got some rest?" asked Flint.

Erik's expression hardened. "No."

"We'll go," said Hass.

"Just let us grab a bite to eat," Ian added.

"Grab it and put it in a sack." Erik threw on his cloak and exited out the back door.

The brothers stared at the door after he closed it.

"Does anyone else get the feeling that Erik has become a little obsessed with finding this girl?" Jamen asked.

"He just wants to do his duty," Flint replied.

Jamen nodded, but Gerall agreed. Something was different. Erik had been searching for the girl for over six months, and for some reason, he refused to tell the parents the girl was dead and to let it go at that.

"Unless you need me, I'm going to head to bathe and sleep," Gerall said.

"You don't want to explain why you have a fine dusting of flour all over your tunic and pants?" asked Jamen.

"Not particularly."

"Was it like a roll in the flour?" Hass picked up two rolls and stuffed them in a bag.

"Since she's a baker and there's no hay." Ian picked up a loaf of bread and a wedge of cheese.

"Yes, I understood your connotation." Gerall pushed his glasses up his nose.

His brothers stared at him.

"No," he finally said. "There wasn't any rolling anywhere."

They chuckled and nodded.

"Goodnight to all of you." Gerall turned and headed out of the solar and up toward his room.

It wasn't like he hadn't wanted to. Heavens above the more time he spent with Eloa, the more he didn't want to be parted from her. Yes, he'd thought about feeling her soft curves pressed against his. To kiss the dip of her throat and glide his tongue down between the swells of her peachy breasts.

He pushed open his bedroom door and quickly stripped his cloak and tunic. The air in the house had become unbearably warm. He opened his window and stood to let the breeze wash over his skin, pebbling it.

He closed his eyes and envisioned Eloa lying in his bed.

Her beautiful chestnut hair spread out over his pillows— her peachy limbs encircling him. The green silk comforter would match her eyes.

Gah! He opened his eyes and scanned his room. He needed to get her out of his head. That wasn't proper to think of a lady like that. She deserved to be treated with respect, not to be fantasied over.

His gaze roamed the room. When had he let it become such a disaster? He moved about systematically picking up his clothes, boots, and books and putting them where they belonged. He spent thirty minutes tidying his room and trying to keep his thoughts off Eloa before finally heading off to bathe. He stood by the tub and imagined Eloa lying in it, covered in bubbles.

Ah, damn. He pinched the bridge of his nose. It would be a cold bath for him tonight. Otherwise, he wouldn't sleep at all.

CHAPTER NINE

Gerall sat with Eloa and his family in front of the stage where a group of townsfolk produced a play, but his eyes weren't on the play, they were on Eloa. He'd gotten up early to help her set up her stand and sell her goods, and then they'd met his family for a picnic and puppet show. She fit into the group like she'd always been there. Playing with the babies and chatting with his sisters-in-law like old friends. She'd especially taken to Zelle, Gerall appreciated her for all the more. Too many of the townsfolk stared at Zelle or whispered about her. Not that she either noticed or cared.

Eloa laughed and clapped her hands at a joke on stage that he missed. But Gerall couldn't seem to tear his gaze away from her. She, like Zelle, didn't seem to care what others thought of her. He didn't know many women that would carry on so well after losing both parents and having no family to rely on. Yet she took to it with hard work and determination. She held an inner strength that even few men possessed.

As if sensing his eyes on her, she looked at him in the setting sunlight. Her green eyes lit like emeralds.

"Would you like to go for a walk?" He couldn't seem to spend enough time with her, getting to know everything about her.

She looked around and then back at the stage before hopping to her feet and helping him up as well. He wanted to keep holding her soft slender hand, but she slipped it away and allowed him to lead.

"Where should we go?"

He hadn't thought that far ahead. "Where would you like to go?"

They started toward the village center. "I've always enjoyed going down to the pond by the mill."

"Truly?" he asked.

"Why not? It's a warm evening. We can dip our feet in the water."

He nodded and followed her across the grass behind the puppet theater. They walked for several minutes, and he enjoyed the tranquil silence that fell between them.

"You are so peaceable," she said.

"Is that a bad thing?"

She shook her head. "When you and your family used to come to town, I could pick you out of all of them within an instant."

"Because I'm the thinnest?"

She laughed. "No. Because your brothers are always so

energetic. So boisterous. But you. You possess a peaceable air."

She used to watch him when he came to town?

"I remember one time when your brothers were rough-housing with the blacksmith's boys. A fight ensued, and you calmly stepped in and ended it with a few sharp words. None of us had ever seen you like that before. The confidence and fierceness you exuded told everyone that you weren't to be trifled with."

He remembered that day. "A boy had punched Kellan in the nose. The wrestling had been good sport, but the boy had punched Kellan for no other reason than to say he'd punched a Gwyn. Kellan was only seven or eight, and bullying is one thing I can't abide."

They turned the corner, and the mill came into view. The smell of grain filling the air.

"You remember a lot about me," he said.

She peeked over at him, and her cheeks deepened a shade. "I admit I was quite lovestruck by you when I was young. After you rescued me with that haypence at the well, I could barely control my tender little heart."

He smiled. "Only a haypence? Well, then what did my gold pieces for the baked goods earn me?"

"A lot of wonderful baked goods."

He laughed. "True. True."

She'd been lovestruck by him when she was a child. He wondered what she felt now.

A family of ducks and several geese swam in the pond, paddling back and forth. Eloa led him down to a grassy spot on the bank, and she slipped off her shoes.

He sat next to her and pulled off his boots and stockings, setting them aside. Eloa scooted forward, tied up her skirt and pushed up her bloomers before walking into the pond. She threw her head back and smiled, letting the setting light shine down on her face.

He watched her for several minutes as she basked in the glow. She turned in a slow circle, and the light illuminated her long slender neck and the swells of her breasts. She stopped turning and looked at him.

"Are you coming in?"

"I'm enjoying the view."

She smiled and then gathered water in her hands and threw it at him. He rolled out of the way, and the water landed on the grass.

"You missed."

She scooped up water again and again threw it at him. He rolled away a second time and determination set on her face. She splashed water at him, and he moved again, but she splashed quicker a second time and hit him square in the face.

He sputtered and wiped his face.

Her eyes widened, and she shook her head. "I'm sorry. I didn't—"

He didn't let her finish her sentence before he leapt to his feet and raced into the water. She squealed and ran the opposite direction. He chased after her, and in her heavy dress and skirt, she slowed and looked back.

"Gerall, I said I'm sorry. Now you better stop. In truth, you better."

He stalked forward despite her words. Eloa smiled and

bit her bottom lip while trying to get away from him. She headed for the edge of the pond and ran out onto the grass once more, and Gerall smiled. He kept his distance just enough to give her the sense that she might get away from him. Then he sprinted after her. She peeked over her shoulder just before he caught her. She shrieked as he grabbed her around the waist and slowed her fall. They tumbled to the ground, and he landed on top of her, both of them laughing.

Her slender form fit underneath his, soft and lush, making his arousal grow. She stopped laughing and smiled up at him. He pushed the hair from her forehead and ran his knuckles across her cheek. She licked her lips, and her eyes stayed on him, wide and hopeful.

Eloa's heart beat so fast she feared Gerall could feel it through her bodice. He stared at her, his face still wet and his glasses dripping from where she'd splashed him. Desire filled his gaze and sent tingles through her. He bent close to her, his lips inches from hers. She shouldn't. She shouldn't get close to him. She should tell him the truth about what she was and let him walk away from her, his reputation still intact. Anything less would end in her pain and possibly his ruination.

He lingered inches above her lips.

"Gerall."

"Yes."

"I need to tell you something."

"Do you?" He rubbed her right earlobe between his thumb and forefinger.

"Yes. Something about me."

"Is it important?"

Her throat dried. "Yes," she whispered.

"Do you want to tell me?"

She didn't want to do anything that might take him away from her. "No."

"Then don't."

She shook her head. "It's not that simple. This thing about me. It… could hurt you. Your family."

He chuckled. "I'm positive that's not true."

"You don't understand."

"I don't need to. Everything I need to know about you I already do. I would consider myself a relatively intelligent man. I'd think that by now, I could judge people pretty well. I doubt there is anything you could tell me that would change my perception of you."

"Even so. I have to tell you."

His eyes grew serious, and he studied her for a moment. "This thing you have to tell me. Is it the reason those two men in town have been eyeing you?"

A chill raced over her skin. If she said no, she'd be lying to him. But if she said yes, it could very well mean his life.

"I… I don't know what you mean."

"I saw them looking at you. Watching you. I saw the fear on your face—"

Eloa sat up suddenly causing Gerall rolled off of her. "I should go."

"Eloa—"

"I have much baking to get done for tomorrow." She jumped to her feet and grabbed her shoes.

"Eloa, please," Gerall called.

She sprinted toward the mill. She couldn't do it. She wouldn't put him in danger. Gerall didn't deserve what would come to him if he became entangled in her mess. She needed to stand on her own two feet.

Her heart cried out for Gerall. She wanted to tell him the truth. The most fantastic feeling of her life had been moments before in his arms. But she refused to be his downfall.

"Hello, Eloa."

She looked up. Charlie leaned against the wall of the mill.

"You and Lord Gwyn seemed to be getting quite cozy in the grass."

She slipped her shoes on and stomped toward town.

"Does he know about you? Did you tell him so that he can protect you and you don't have to pay? Did you give yourself to him?"

Eloa stopped moving. Rage coursed through her.

"You know it doesn't have to be like this. I know what you are, and I don't care," he continued.

She spun around. "Stay away from me, Charlie. Trust me; I'm not the pretty sparrow you think I am."

He advanced, looking her up and down. "Aren't you now? You look like no more than a pretty sparrow. And pretty sparrow, I could protect you from Trent. From the others in town."

Something was going on. If she could get information, maybe she could help Gerall.

"So, you're saying that if I give in to you, you'll keep me safe? I won't have to pay the gold piece a week?" She stepped closer to him, and he smiled, revealing crooked teeth.

"I'd be sure of it." He ran his hand down her arm.

Bile rose in her throat, but she kept the smile on her face. "And who would you keep me safe from?"

"Trent."

"So, it's Trent who runs the racket of protection for the shop owners?" She touched his chest as he rested his hand on her hip.

"Of course not. We're second in charge."

She rubbed a circle on his chest as he moved closer. "And who is in charge?"

He smiled at her again and then his eyes steeled. He grabbed her hips and dragged her in contact with him.

"You don't need to know that."

She let her smile drop. "Let go of me."

"What? Suddenly passing me over now that you know I'm not the head man?"

"I said to let go. If you don't, you won't like the outcome."

"Oh, really? I like a good fight."

"So do I." Gerall stepped out of the shadows and pulled Charlie's hand from Eloa's body.

"Gerall, don't!" she cried.

Charlie gave a loathsome grin and pulled a dagger from his waistband. "You shouldn't have done that."

"No," said Gerall. "I really think I should have."

Eloa stepped in the way and put her hand up to stop Charlie. "Stop. It's me you want."

"Not anymore." Charlie pushed her out of the way.

Eloa stumbled and hit the side of the mill.

"Don't touch her," Gerall growled

"When I'm done with you, I'll do more than touch her." Charlie lunged at Gerall and Eloa screamed.

Gerall spun out of the way faster than she could see. He stuck out his leg, tripping Charlie. Charlie stumbled forward, and Gerall kicked him in the rear.

"You don't want to do this," said Gerall. "Stop now, and I promise I won't hurt you. I'll just take you to my brothers to answer some questions."

Charlie spun around. "You can't question me if you're dead."

He ran at Gerall again, and Gerall went to spin out of the way, but Charlie met him head-on. He slashed with his knife opening Gerall's tunic with a quick strike.

Gerall backed up and grabbed his stomach. Blood seeped through the fabric staining it red.

Eloa took a step forward. "Gerall!"

Charlie advanced, stabbing at Gerall's gut again, but Gerall grabbed the knife and twisted it out of Charlie's hands, flinging it to the ground. He punched Charlie in the face with several quick strikes. Charlie doubled over, and Gerall kneed him in the gut twice.

Charlie fell to the ground, and Gerall kicked him in the face. Gerall lost his footing, and his glasses flew from his face, landing several feet away. Charlie fell backward, sprawled on the ground. Gerall jumped on top of him, punching him in the face until Charlie's body went limp.

Eloa ran forward and grabbed Gerall's arm. "Gerall, stop. He's down."

Gerall looked at her, his eyes focused in a way she'd only seen when he'd broken up that fight when they were kids.

He took a deep breath and grabbed his stomach. Blood drenched the entire front of his tunic. Eloa caught him as he fell off Charlie.

Eloa moved his hands to look at the wound.

"Guess I'm a bit rustier than I thought," he breathed. "Go get my brothers, please."

She lifted his tunic and gasped. The wound was deep enough that she could see the layers beneath his skin. Her stomach turned, and she fought the urge to throw up.

"This is bad." Guilt raced through her, and tears dripped from her eyes. "Why did you do that? He could have killed you."

"You'd have been worth it."

She shook her head. "No. I'm not. You don't know." She continued to shake her head as blood poured through her fingers. No. This could not be happening. She couldn't let him die. She couldn't.

"Get my brothers. They can fix me."

"No. You'll bleed out while I'm gone."

He tried to lift his head to look.

"Lay still." She couldn't sit on her rear and let him die. She had to do something. Her gut clenched. She could heal him. But if she did...

She looked deep into his eyes. "I'm sorry," she said.

"For what?"

"For not telling you sooner."

"Telling me what?"

Eloa looked at her hands and pulled her magick from deep within. She focused on Gerall's wound and forced her magick through her palms to his skin. She willed the magick to fix him. A moment passed and then the blood beneath her fingers staunched. The skin knit slowly back together, leaving a long, puckered scar.

Eloa sucked in a deep breath. Every muscle in her body ached, and her eyelids drooped with fatigue. She'd not used that much magick in her life.

Gerall sat up, his eyes wide. She dropped her gaze to her shaking hands. What would he say? Would he turn on her? Kick her out of Westfall? She sucked in a breath and waited.

Gerall reached out and pushed her hair from her ear and ran his fingers up the rim of it to the tip. She resisted looking at him. She couldn't bear to see his face.

"Eloa. Look at me." He pulled her chin so that she faced him again, but she wouldn't lift her eyes.

He cupped her face in his calloused hands, and her chest squeezed tighter than a corset. She finally lifted her gaze and looked into his gentle face.

She opened her mouth to explain, but before she could say anything, his lips pressed against hers softly.

Pure white energy rolled through her body, warming every inch of her from the inside out. Her heart thundered, and he released her mouth and smiled.

"You're fae," he said. "That's what they have over you, isn't it?"

She nodded and searched his face.

"All right. Get my brothers. I'll wait here with Charlie. We're going to fix this. Don't worry."

"You... you don't hate me?"

He chuckled. "I'd be a hypocrite if I did."

What did that mean? "What about your brothers? Will they—"

"They won't bat an eye." He brushed her hair from her face. "Go. Swiftly. I'm going to need their help getting Charlie back to the manor house without the whole town seeing us."

She pushed to her feet and brushed off her dress. "Don't go anywhere."

He pressed his hand to his stomach. "Trust me. I'm not."

Eloa looked to Charlie and then ran over and grabbed his knife and Gerall's glasses and dropped them in his lap.

"I'll be back in a minute." Eloa hitched up her skirt and headed back for the green.

A weight lifted off her shoulders, making her smile. He hadn't even cared she was half-fae. More than that, he'd kissed her. Gerall Gwyn had kissed her.

CHAPTER TEN

A half-fae. It explained a lot. Her slightly more than beautiful face. The grace in the way she moved. Her gentle yet stubborn nature. The way she feared letting anyone too close. And Gerall warmed at the knowledge that it wasn't just that she didn't want him.

He tried pushing to his feet but slipped and fell again, his head too light to think straight. His stomach ached from the wound, though Eloa had been able to close it. The muscles burned every time he breathed, shooting pain up over his chest. But at least the bleeding had stopped. He wouldn't admit it to Eloa, but he hadn't been so sure he would make it until she brought back his brothers. If she hadn't closed the wound… who knew what might have happened.

Having grown up in Westfall, he couldn't believe that Eloa had learned much about how to use her magick. Not like those who lived in Ville DeFee. How lonely she had to have been these last months since her father's death. Being all alone in a town where she feared being outed at every turn. How frightened she must have been. And yet, still so strong.

Footsteps raced his direction, and Gerall grabbed the knife, gripping it tight. Three men ran around the mill, and he brandished the blade, but it was just his brothers and Adrian. Flint ran to his side, and he and Adrian helped Gerall to his feet.

"Are you all right?" asked Flint, his eyes searching Gerall's face through his red glasses.

"I'll be fine."

"What happened?" demanded Jamen.

"I believe I found a link to what's been going on in Westfall. We just need to question him." Flint and Adrian helped him walk as Jamen checked on Charlie. "Where's Eloa?"

"With Zelle and Scarlet. She's covered in your blood, so they wrapped her in a blanket and took her to the carriage. They should be here any minute."

Gerall needed to get her out of Westfall. At least for the night, he needed to know she was somewhere safe.

Flint pressed his hand to Gerall's stomach, making him wince. "You're not bleeding."

He shook his head. "She healed me. Or at least closed the wound."

Flint nodded. "Zelle said she was special. Fae?"

"Half," Gerall replied.

"We need to get moving," said Jamen. "This guy isn't going to stay out for long."

Adrian released Gerall and walked to Charlie. "I'll take him to the road outside town. Meet me there."

"Are you sure?" asked Jamen. "This isn't your problem."

Adrian sniffed Charlie. "I have a feeling this is directly related to my problem."

Flint nodded. "We'll meet you in twenty minutes."

Adrian hefted Charlie over his shoulders and headed back toward the pond.

"That's a long trek heading back through the woods," said Gerall.

Flint shifted Gerall's weight on his shoulder, and Jamen came up the other side and helped out. "He knows what he's doing."

Gerall shook his head. "I feel like a baby letting you two help me."

"Trust me," said Jamen. "You've carried us plenty of times. It's good to finally see you aren't perfect."

Gerall chuckled. "Well, it's embarrassing that a common thug wounded me."

"Yes, how did that happen?" asked Flint.

"Too much time with animals and not enough training with us," replied Jamen.

"Who knew we'd still need the skills?" asked Gerall.

"We'll always need them." Flint's voice held a heavy edge to it.

With the problems in Westfall and Fairelle in general, the violence wasn't bound to end soon. And if he planned on trying to make a life with Eloa, it might never end. Maybe he did need to spend more of his time training.

The sound of hoofbeats clopped toward them and

then their carriage pulled around the mill. With Scarlet at the reins, Jamen let go of Gerall quickly and ran to the coach.

"Scarlet!" He jumped up and took the reins from her.

"Don't you even think about it," she replied. "I rode horses until the week before our son Kellan was born. I can drive a carriage just fine in my condition."

"Of course you can, but you don't need to. I'm here."

She rolled her eyes. "My hero."

Zelle and Eloa exited the carriage, and Eloa ran for Gerall.

"How are you?" She shouldered his weight.

"I'll live, thanks to you."

She smiled and together she and Flint helped him to the carriage. Flint opened the door, and Gerall climbed in and sat on the pillow-covered bench. He ached from his waist to his shoulders.

"Uncle Gerall, you're bleeding." His nephew Kellan pointed at him.

Gerall put on his best smile. "It's not bad, little one."

Flint helped Zelle inside, and Jamen finally convinced Scarlet to ride inside as well. Zelle and Scarlet picked up their babies and sat them on their laps.

Eloa stood outside the carriage, her face full of worry. "I should get back to my shop."

"No," said Gerall. "You need to come with us."

"He's right," said Jamen. "With Charlie going missing, they could come looking for you tonight."

"Even more reason why," she said. "I can't let anything happen to my— bakery."

"You really should come with us," said Gerall. "I don't want to chance anything happening to you."

She shook her head. "I can't."

Stubborn fae. Gerall breathed deep and slid to the door. "Then I'm staying too."

"Gerall—"

"You can rebuild a store, but not if you're dead." He looked at her hard, and she bit her lip. She looked between them all, and finally, her shoulders slumped.

Without a word, she hopped up into the carriage.

"I'll get the horses and be right behind you," Jamen said.

Flint nodded, closed the door, and then hopped up to the driver's seat.

Gerall wrapped his arm around Eloa's shoulders, and she lay her head on his chest. Gerall looked over at his sisters-in-law, who both tried not to stare, but their suppressed smiles were more than obvious. Gerall shook his head. His sisters-in-law were just as bad as their husbands.

Eloa's gut twisted in knots riding in the carriage with the Gwyns. As much as she relished the idea of being with them, especially Gerall, the anxiety that engulfed her at the thought that her father might be harmed grated on her. The all-consuming guilt for leaving him behind threatened to have her jumping out of the carriage. But if she went back and told him what had happened, he would never let her hear the end of it for not going with Gerall.

She looked into Gerall's face. He leaned back against the seat, eyes closed, skin waxy and pale. She'd been able to close the wound, but that hadn't done much for his excessive blood loss, and she wasn't sure how much of his insides she'd repaired. She'd never healed someone like that before. Sure, she'd helped her father with his burns, but even those had only gone so deep. Gerall's wound had been much worse.

The carriage pulled to a stop, and Eloa looked out the window. They couldn't possibly be there yet. A large, dark-haired man stood in the road with someone over his shoulder.

Jamen trotted his horse and a second one forward. The large man threw the unconscious one over the back of his horse. *Charlie.* The large man got on the horse, and he and Jamen led the way.

"What are they doing with Charlie?" she asked Gerall.

"We need to question him. See what he knows."

Eloa shook her head. "But this is my problem, not yours."

"Unfortunately, this goes deeper than you know. Something is going on in Westfall, and we believe Charlie is low on the chain of command, but we need to find out who is in charge and stop them before they cause a full-blown panic in the town."

"Panic over what?"

Gerall looked at Zelle and Scarlet.

"Let's get back to the manor house and settle Gerall, then we can discuss it further," said Zelle.

The coach moved forward again, and Eloa stared out

the window. There was something about the Gwyns she didn't know, and for the first time, a niggling of fear washed through her.

Eloa had never seen Gwyn Manor before. She'd never seen any manor house before, so she had nothing to compare it to. But an impressive and imposing stone structure, it loomed over them, making her wonder for the first time in a long time what the castle in Ville DeFee looked like.

The coach pulled around the side, past an aviary full of birds that cooed and squawked. A half-alive flower garden came into view as they rounded the back of the house toward a large stable. They stopped, and the coach dipped back and forth as Flint jumped to the ground. He came around to Gerall's side and pulled open the door. His eyes moved behind the strange red glasses, but she got the feeling he couldn't see well. He tenderly touched Gerall's head in a way that she'd not attributed to his character before.

"I'm alive," Gerall said without opening his eyes.

Flint reached in, pulling Gerall's arm over his shoulder.

"I can't lose another brother," he said softly.

Gerall's eyes opened, and for a moment, the two shared a heavy look. "I've got too much pride to allow myself to be killed by the likes of him."

Flint helped Gerall out of the coach, and Jamen ran up to meet them. Together the brothers half-carried Gerall to the back door and inside the house.

The large dark-haired man she didn't recognize lumbered over to the coach and took Jamen's son from Scarlet before helping her out of the coach.

"Thank you, Adrian," she said.

He inclined his head, but didn't reply.

Scarlet took her son and dropped him to his feet. Taking his hand, the two waddled to the door.

Adrian helped Zelle and the twins out of the coach and then Eloa. Magick wafted off him as he took her hand, but she couldn't place it.

She stepped from the carriage and noticed Adrian staring down at her.

"You aren't human," he said.

She gave him a tight smile. "Neither are you."

He nodded. "Werewolf."

A chill ran through her. So, there were werewolves.

"Fae."

He nodded. "I better get back to my charge before he awakens."

He stomped back to the horses that waited by the stable door, and lead them inside the stable.

"Gerall's resting in his room."

Eloa jumped at the sound of Flint's voice. She turned to the brother who loomed over her.

He stared at her like he wanted to say something, but he didn't speak.

She headed for the door when he caught her hand and then pulled away instantly.

"I'm sorry. I just... I wanted to thank you. For saving my brother."

"Wouldn't anyone have done the same?"

"Given what you were exposing about yourself? No, I don't believe they would have."

So, they all knew. The idea comforted and scared her at the same time. But given they kept company with a werewolf, she was beginning to believe Gerall's words. "*They won't bat an eye.*"

"Thank you for welcoming me into your home. I don't want to bring you any more unneeded pressure."

Flint licked his lips as if choosing his words carefully. "It seems we collect those like us. Those who don't quite fit in anywhere else."

Jamen joined them. "Is Adrian in the stable?"

"I believe so."

"What are you going to do to Charlie?" Eloa asked.

The brothers looked between each other and then at her.

"Whatever we have to," said Flint.

She wanted to ask what that meant, but she didn't need to. The look on Flint's face said it all.

"I'm going to go inside and check on Gerall."

"Please do," said Flint.

"Our wives are inside setting up your bath and getting you fresh clothes," said Jamen.

Eloa looked down at her gown, realizing how stiff it had become from the dirt and blood.

"Thank you," said Eloa. "For everything."

Jamen smiled, making his eyes crinkle in the corners and lighting up his features in a way she'd never seen him do before.

"You are most welcome," he replied.

Warmth spread through her at the compassion and

friendliness they all showed her. She'd never had people treat her with such kindness before.

Eloa turned and headed for the house as Jamen and Flint unhooked the horses from the carriage and walking them into the stable.

Her gut clenched as she thought of Charlie and what they might do to him, but surprisingly, she didn't pity him one ounce.

Eloa entered the large room filled with a huge table, chairs as well as a fireplace and looked around. In the middle of the table sat two of her loaves of bread and some butter. Her stomach growled. She'd not eaten since that morning.

"You're welcome to some bread," said Scarlet, entering the room. "You did make it after all."

"Yes, but you paid for it."

Scarlet waved her hand at Eloa. "Everyone shares around here. This dress was Zelle's when she was pregnant with the twins and had been Mother Gwyn's before that. The beds we sleep in have been in the family for a century. Even this manor house has been in the Gwyn family for longer than has been recorded. In the Gwyn family, if it belongs to one, it belongs to all. Well, most things anyway. I don't want you to think we are into swapping beds or anything torrid like that."

Eloa walked to the table and cut a slice of bread. "So, the oldest brother, Erik, he doesn't mind sharing all he has?"

Scarlet snorted. "Erik is more than happy to share what he's been given because they all share the responsibilities. Gerall helps with the tenants. Jamen and I help with the stable. Zelle does most of the cooking. Hass and Ian help with the babies. We all do the cleaning. Providing and Lording over Westfall is a family affair."

Eloa bit into the bread. "It's wonderful to have so many people you care about so close by. But do you wish you had your own space?"

Scarlet rubbed her belly. "Every once in a while. But the house is big enough, and there's always weekends away when we need to breathe."

"Where do you go when you get out?"

Scarlet shrugged. "Tanah Darah. Westfall Inn. Aunt Violet's house. Ville DeFee."

"Ville DeFee?" The thought of being able to visit the Faelands lifted her spirits.

"Queen Cinder is a family friend."

Eloa shook her head. "Werewolves? Fae Queens? There really is more to you Gwyns than anyone knows, isn't there?"

Scarlet stopped. "I think maybe I better let Gerall tell the rest. Come, let's get you in a bath and out of those clothes. I know he's anxious to see you."

Eloa swallowed the rest of her bread. "And I him."

Scarlet nodded and led her out of the solar and into a large foyer. An ornate wooden staircase stood to one side. The women ascended the stairs and halfway up, Scarlet stopped and grabbed the railing.

"Are you all right?" asked Eloa.

Scarlet took a deep, steadying breath and grimaced.

"Should I get someone?" asked Eloa. "Jamen's in the stable."

"No." Scarlet took another deep breath and then straightened. "I'm fine." She breathed a few more times and then smiled.

"How much longer?"

"At least another month." Scarlet started up the stairs again, this time holding her belly.

"Are you hoping for another boy?"

Scarlet turned and gave a sad smile. "No. A girl. Jamen wants a girl so badly. We love little Kellan, but I think it would ease his heart if this one is a girl."

Eloa wondered what Scarlet's words meant, but she hadn't the heart to pry.

Scarlet crossed the landing to a bedroom down at the end and pushed open the door. The beautiful room was more ornate than any Eloa had ever seen. So large that almost her entire hut could have fit into it.

"This is Snow's room. She doesn't live here anymore though, so you are welcome to it while you're here."

Eloa looked around the room. "It's so nice. Are you sure it's not a problem for me to stay in here? The brothers won't mind?"

Scarlet shook her head. "No one will mind at all. Not even Snow."

Eloa studied Scarlet for a minute. She'd seen the woman around town but had never really gotten to know her.

"I have to be honest," Eloa said. "You have all been so much more accommodating and welcoming than I ever could have hoped for. I'm not sure what to say. I've never been greeted with such hospitality. Is it because Erik is Lord and has to be hospitable? I don't want you to feel like this is charity."

"It is charity," said Scarlet. "But not the way you think. We are kind and hospitable because Gerall has chosen to let you into our lives. He is smart, the smartest of all of them to be honest, and I doubt very highly he would have brought you here if he didn't believe he could trust you and if he did not care for you quite a bit. We aren't kind to you because it's our duty. We are kind to you because it's who we are."

Shame heated Eloa's cheeks for having thought they were only friendly because they had to be. But she wasn't used to anyone in town being nice to her because they could. Far from it, she found them more likely to be falsely nice if they wanted something and ignorant if they didn't.

"There are towels in the bathing room down the hall and some room temperature water in there as well. I'm sorry Hass and Ian aren't here to bring up hot water for you."

"Where are they and Erik?"

Scarlet smiled and pointed to the bed, where an elegant, beige embroidered dress lay. "Feel free to use that. I'm pretty sure it will fit you."

Scarlet walked out the door and down the hallway. Eloa looked around the room once more and then to the dress. She could use a bath. She couldn't remember ever having one in a tub before.

CHAPTER ELEVEN

Gerall lay in bed, the pain in his chest refusing to subside. The tightness and shortness of breath made him unable to get comfortable. A gentle knock on the door pulled his attention.

"Come in."

The door opened, and Eloa stood in a clean, fresh dress he'd remembered Snow wearing before. He smiled at her, and she smiled in return.

"Hi."

"Hello." She stood in the doorway as though not sure if she should enter.

Gerall waved her in, and she stepped inside, closing the door behind her. She took in the room as if unsure of what to do next.

"Do you want to sit—" Before he could offer her a chair, she joined him on the edge of his bed. The scent of the soap lingered on her skin, making him itch to pull her closer and hold her tight.

"How are you feeling?"

He pushed his glasses up his nose. "Better, thank you."

Eloa took him in, and he realized that he wore no tunic. His sheets lay low across his torso, and for a moment, he fought the desire to make himself more presentable.

"Do you mind if I look?" she asked, motioning to his stomach.

Gerall nodded, and she scooted closer to him. She pulled down the sheets and duvet, revealing his stomach and hips. She ran her slender fingers over the angry red scar on his belly.

"Does that hurt?"

He shook his head, but his throat dried at her touch. "My chest is tight, and it's a bit hard to breathe, but I think I'm good."

"I've never tried to heal someone that extensively before."

"I can't imagine you've used your magick much since you live among humans."

She inspected her fingernails. "I've been using it quite a lot in the last months, to be honest."

"Really?"

Her cheeks flushed with a beautiful pink blush. "I... I've been using my magick on my baked goods. I didn't mean any harm," she said quickly. "We'd just been barely scraping by for so long that I thought if I just used a little magick to enhance my goods, maybe we would get more customers.

Enough to possibly afford a bit more. Not a lot mind you, just... something."

Her gaze dropped to her hands again, and Gerall couldn't help but smile. He tipped her chin up with his fingers.

"If magick is what makes your food taste so exceptional, then you can use it all you want."

Her expression relaxed. "Will you tell me something?"

"Anything."

"You are human."

"Yes." A chill ran over him as he knew where her questioning would lead.

"But... you are friends with a werewolf and you know the queen of Ville DeFee. How is that possible?"

"It's a rather long tale."

She pulled her legs under herself and folded her hands in her lap. "I'm not going anywhere tonight."

Gerall nodded. Where did he start? "After my parents died, a woman— we don't know who— placed a mantle upon my brothers and I. It had to do with the Fairelle prophecies. She made us vampire hunters."

"Vampire hunters?" Her eyes rounded in surprise.

"We hunted them and kept them out of Westfall. They live in Tanah Darah, north of Wolvenglen forest."

She looked to the side as if remembering something. "Scarlet said you go to Tanah Darah when you need some time to yourself."

He nodded. "Yes. Our sister, Snow, is married to the King of Tanah Darah, Sageren."

"So, he's a vampire? But you just said you kill vampires."

"It's... complicated. But yes, we do. Ones that hunt humans."

"You know fae, vampires, and werewolves?"

"Daemons and a werebear and dragons as well. A mage too, as it turns out."

She sat silently digested the information. "So those do all exist."

Gerall lifted his hand and touched her cheek. "Believe it or not, most of them are good people, just like us. And if you'll let me, I'll protect you from the rest."

Her gaze met his, and his heart hammered.

"Are... are you asking me to marry you?" she stammered.

Was he? They'd only been getting to know each other for the past week. But he'd honestly never felt anything for a woman before. She intrigued him and made him laugh and challenged him. Yes, he decided. He wanted to be with her.

"I... suppose I am."

She blinked several times.

"You don't have to answer me now," he said. "But I want you to know my intentions. This isn't just a passing fancy for me. The way I feel about you—"

"I feel the same."

Gerall couldn't hold back the smile that spread across his face. He pulled her gently until her lips met his. Her warm arms slid up his chest and her body pressed against his, making him light with desire.

He parted her lips with his, and their tongues swirled together. He pulled her closer, and her hips rested on his. The wound on his abdomen ached at the pressure of her weight, so he rolled her on her back. He stopped momentarily to make sure she still wanted to continue, but she pulled his mouth back to hers and wrapped her arms around his neck.

Gerall's hand ran down the side of her dress to her leg. He kissed her cheek and then over to her ear. Her body arched against his, and he kissed up to the tip of her ear. Her nails dug into his shoulders, and he stopped.

"Am I hurting you?"

She shook her head, her breathing coming in and out in shallow bursts. "My- my ears are sensitive."

Were they? He leaned in and breathed on her throat, licking her skin, tasting her sweet perfume. She smelled of spices and herbs. He kissed up to her ear again and then delicately ran his tongue along the edge of it to the short-pointed tip. She moaned into his chest, and her hands moved down his body to his rear. She clutched at him, making him harden and the need to be inside her spike.

He kissed down her throat to the tops of her firm breasts. He kissed over them gently as he slid his hand under the hem of her dress.

"Gerall," she whispered his name.

"Do you want to stop?"

She shook her head, vehemently. "I want to be your wife."

Happiness spread through him like brush fire. "If you want to wait, we can wait. We don't have to do this now."

She kissed him hard. "If we don't do it now, I fear I might burst." She kissed him again. "Make love to me."

He looked deep into her emerald. "I- I need you to

know. I've never... I mean, I'm not... I haven't been with a woman before."

"Neither have I." She laughed. "I mean, with a man. Or a woman. I mean..." Her cheeks flushed a deep rose color.

He kissed her softly. "I know what you mean."

He ran his hand up her thigh to the waistband of her pantaloons. Lifting himself off her, he slowly pulled them down and shoved them into the recesses of his blankets. He undid the buttons of her overdress, one by one, kissing his way down her torso. He wanted to savor every moment of this with her. Remember every detail of their first time. He pushed the overdress off of her and then slid her chemise up her body. Right before he revealed her breasts, she grabbed his hand, and he stopped.

"As I said, we can wait if you aren't ready."

She looked deep into his eyes. "I just... I don't want you to change your mind."

He caressed her cheek. Nothing he said would fully take away her fear. Sex, when not married, could ruin her. He knew that fear all too well for women in Fairelle. He breathed in, and his chest felt tighter than ever.

"Let's wait. I can call my brother Erik to the house within the next day. He could be here and marry us, and then you wouldn't have to worry."

"Call him?"

"We have a magick mirror we use to communicate."

She chuckled. "Of course you do." Eloa moved his hand from her chemise and raised her chemise over her head and flung it to the floor. "I don't want to wait that long."

He looked down at her beautiful body— flawless soft

skin, slim waist that curved into slender hips. His body pulsed with need, and it took all of his restraint to keep things gentle.

Her slender fingers glided down to his pants, and she deftly undid the tie at his waist. Their eyes stayed locked on each other as she slid his pants down over his hips and then ran her palms over his backside. He dipped down and kissed her mouth, his body aching and hot.

"Eloa. I want you."

Eloa's body thrummed with need. She'd waited so many years to be in Gerall's arms, and she could hardly believe she wasn't dreaming. His hands and mouth caressed her body, making it tingle in ways she'd never experienced before. She ran her hands over the long scar on his abdomen, and his muscles quaked beneath her touch.

"Am I hurting you?" she asked.

"I've had far worse before."

"If you want to wait until you have your strength back—"

"I have all I require."

She wanted him, but a part of her still feared what might happen. If he changed his mind, she'd be both an outcast and used. She didn't know if she could get past that. But she also knew him. He wasn't like that. She knew that with him, she finally felt safe.

Eloa reached down and stroked his length, making him shudder. He eased her legs further apart with his thighs and then swirled his palm against her sensitive opening. She moaned and pushed closer to his hand as she stroked him long and soft.

He rubbed against her over and over, sending sensations and shockwaves through her body. Slowly he pressed his fingers against her opening and slid them inside her. Her body clenched around him at the strange and pleasurable feel. She moved his body closer to hers. He removed his fingers, kissing her as he guided himself against her. She kissed him hard and held onto his hips as he pressed inside slowly. Once their bodies joined, he kissed her and lay still for a moment allowing her to adjust. He brushed her hair with his fingers and kissed all over her face.

"You are so beautiful, Eloa."

"So are you." She wanted to sound loving and sincere, but she felt silly, having said it.

He chuckled.

He pulled his hips back, and the friction between their bodies made her skin pebble with goosebumps.

He bent and kissed her breasts in turn. Licking her nipples and making them pinch tight. She grabbed his hips and guided him deeper. He picked up a rhythm, and soon their bodies joined in a soft, love-filled blending.

His thrusts grew faster, and she found herself pulling him into her harder, wanting to feel all of him. His eyes closed, and his head drew back. A pained expression crossed his face, and before she could ask him if he was all right, his breathing quickened, and he called her name. She hung onto him, rocking him through his climax. His lean muscles pulled tight, and he gasped as his body arched, and then he gasped again and again like he couldn't catch his breath.

"Gerall?"

He tried to breathe in as a look of panic crossed on his face.

She rolled him on his back, unlocking their bodies. "Gerall?"

He sucked in a breath and coughed. The coughing spasmed, and he grabbed his chest.

"Gerall!" Panic swept over her.

He coughed again, and blood splattered her face.

"GERALL!" ELOA SCREAMED AND KNELT BY HIS SIDE. HER face swam in and out of view as he fought to stay conscious.

The coughing ripped at his insides like shards of glass. He hacked and fought to breathe. Eloa rolled him on his side and whacked him on the back.

"Gerall. Gerall?"

He couldn't answer as he tried to suck air into his lungs, but fluid filled his throat and mouth as if he were drowning. The coughing turned to choking.

Eloa's eyes widened in alarm. "You're bleeding." She grabbed her chemise and yanked it on, racing for the door she screamed for help as every muscle in Gerall's chest tightened and pounding resonated in his head. Blood spewed out of his mouth once more.

"Help!" Eloa screamed. "Zelle!"

She ran back to the bed and covered him with a sheet.

Footsteps ran toward the door, and Zelle pushed into the room and headed straight for Gerall. He opened his mouth and closed it again, trying to tell her how he felt, but only blood bubbled out of his mouth.

"What the—" Scarlet stood in the doorway. "Oh my."

"Go to the window," ordered Zelle. "Yell for Flint. Go!"

Scarlet waddled out of the room.

"You." Zelle turned to Eloa. "Help me."

Eloa knelt by Gerall, her face pale and strained. His vision began to blur, and darkness tinged the edges of his sight. He tried to keep awake as his chest tightened like his horse had decided to use him as a footstool.

"Is all this blood his? Where is he bleeding from?" Zelle looked him over.

Eloa's cheeks flushed. "Most of it's... mine."

Zelle scanned them both, assessing the situation, and nodded.

"You missed something when you healed him," said Zelle. "You need to find it and fix it."

"I- I- I don't know what to do. I- I've never done this before." The fear in Eloa's voice made Gerall want to comfort her.

Please, gods, do not let him die. Not now. Not when he'd finally found the one he wanted to be with. If he died, she would never forgive herself.

"You can do this." Zelle's voice softened. "Here."

Eloa's palms touched Gerall's stomach. The darkness crept closer and closer, blotting out her beautiful face.

"Use your magick to find it. Feel inside him. Find the problem. You can do this."

Warmth spread through Gerall's belly as Eloa's shaking palms ran over his skin. When she hit the spot where the sharp pain twisted inside him, he grabbed her arm.

"There," said Zelle. "That has to be it."

Darkness obscured his vision, and Gerall's hand fell from Eloa's arm as the pounding in his head and chest grew to the point of exploding. *This is it. The moment I died.* He hadn't even gotten the chance to tell her he loved her.

Don't die. Don't die. Don't die. Eloa's hands shook, and she tried to concentrate her magick.

Heavy footsteps rushed into the room.

"What happened?" Flint ran to the bed. "Gerall. Gerall, wake up." He shook Gerall's shoulder. "By the gods where is all this blood from?"

Eloa refused to allow her mortification to break her concentration. It couldn't be any more embarrassing if she hung the bloodied sheets out the window for every passerby to see what they'd done.

"Where's he bleeding from?" Flint demanded. "We need to stop—"

"Stop!" Eloa shouted. "I'm trying to concentrate."

"Flint," Zelle whispered. "It's not *all* his." Eloa didn't need to look at them to tell the silent conversation passing between them. But she had no time to even think about that.

"You can do this," Zelle said soothingly. "You can find it."

Eloa reached inside Gerall with her magick and pushed through his body, trying to locate the problem. She finally found it. A change in the feel of his body. A space where there shouldn't be one. The left side of his chest caved in slightly. His lung. Something about his lung. She pushed at it with her magick, forcing the organ to mend.

Air. She had to get air into him. She wracked her mind for something to do and finally, desperately, leaned over him and tried to breathe into his mouth. Nothing happened.

"What are you doing?" Flint asked.

"He needs air, but I can't get any into him." She leaned back and felt inside him with her magick again. Everything inside felt wet and sticky. "He's bleeding inside." She pressed her hands to his lungs again. They'd filled up with blood. She pushed her magick into the blood in his abdomen and forced it to dry up. Tracing her hands up his chest, she pulled the blood from his body, forcing it out of his mouth. The dark liquid poured out of him onto the sheets, staining them further.

"Help me turn him." She climbed off him, and Flint rolled Gerall onto his side. Jamen climbed on the bed next to her and moved behind Gerall, propping him up. More and more, she pushed the blood out of him, running her hands higher and higher until everything came out.

"Roll him back," she said.

She climbed up, straddling his hips.

"What are you doing? Flint asked.

She looked up at him. "Back away. Everyone. You can't be touching him."

Concern crossed their features, but she had no time for it.

"Come away, Love." Zelle pulled Flint away from Gerall. Jamen backed up off the bed.

"Please let this work. Please let this work," she whispered. Eloa placed her hands directly over Gerall's heart. She stared into his pale and waxy face. She needed him to wake. She needed him to be all right. She... needed him.

Drawing all the magick she had left in her, she focused it toward Gerall's chest. She balled it in tighter and tighter, the energy building until she thought her hands might explode. They glowed bright white and then she pressed down on his chest at the same moment she let her magick go. The energy slammed into his chest, lifting him off the bed. His eyes flew wide, and he sucked in a gulping breath. He grabbed onto her legs and dropped back to the bed. Eloa wrapped her hands around his as his fingers dug deep into her skin. She laughed as tears flowed from her eyes. He lived.

His gaze connected with hers as he continued to suck air in.

Flint raced over. "Gerall? You all right?"

He looked to Flint and nodded.

"Is he really all right?" Flint asked her.

"I... I think so."

"You think so?"

Zelle laid her hand on Flint's arm. "She is doing her best. She isn't a healer."

"But she has magick."

"Yes, magick, I am assuming she hasn't been taught to use properly."

Flint turned to Eloa and inclined his head. "I apologize. I didn't mean any disrespect."

Eloa nodded as fatigue washed over her. She suddenly became acutely aware of her placement atop Gerall's half-naked body. She slid off him, and he took her hand in his and squeezed it tight.

"Thank you."

She gave him a weak smile.

"He's too weak," she said. "We have to do something about the blood loss."

"What do we need to do?" asked Jamen.

Eloa shook her head. "I do not know."

"He needs to replenish his blood," said Scarlet. "Even with your family's quick healing ability, he needs more."

"I can cook some beef stock and bone broth," said Zelle.

Flint nodded. "That's a good idea."

"Are you sure you are all right?" asked Jamen.

Eloa looked at Gerall's face, which was as close to a deathly pall as she'd ever seen a man.

"I just need sleep," Gerall managed. "And some water."

"I'll get some." Scarlet walked out.

The group stared at Gerall for a minute and then Zelle pulled on Flint's hand.

"I'm going to make the broth. Get them some fresh sheets, and you and Jamen put them on the bed."

"I can do it," said Eloa quickly.

"Nonsense," replied Zelle. "You wash up, and we'll get

you another chemise. Then you and Gerall can rest. I'm sure with all that exertion you are almost dead on your feet."

Zelle wasn't going to take no for an answer, so Eloa nodded and slid from the bed. Gerall held her hand for a moment longer.

"I'm not leaving," she said.

"Neither am I," he replied.

She wished that they were alone to share the intimate moment, but that wasn't going to happen right then. So Eloa followed Zelle toward a bedroom at the end of the hall and Zelle pushed open the door into the richly furnished room. She walked to a far corner and opened a large wardrobe. Pushing several dresses aside, she plucked out two beautiful gowns and two chemises and handed them to Eloa. Eloa's gaze traveled over the dresses.

"I... I can't take your dresses. They're too fine."

Zelle smiled. "They aren't mine. They were Mother Gwyn's. They're yours now."

"No. I... I couldn't possibly."

Zelle pushed the garments into Eloa's arms. "Yes you can. You're a Lady Gwyn now too. Everything we have is yours."

"But... we aren't even married yet."

Zelle chuckled. "Trust me, as far as this family is concerned you are."

CHAPTER TWELVE

Gerall spent the next twelve hours sipping broth and cuddling next to Eloa, but by morning, his body had begun to chill and sweat at the same time, and he couldn't stomach any more of the broth.

"I think it's an infection," Eloa told Jamen and Flint. "It could be that the knife was dirty, or..."

"Or?" asked Jamen.

She looked over at him, and Gerall blinked his bleary eyes.

"Poison," she whispered.

"I can hear just fine," Gerall croaked. "You don't need to whisper."

The three walked to his bed, and Eloa sat and took his clammy hand in hers.

"What do you think?" Flint asked him.

"Rapid heartbeat, shallow breathing, pain in my joints

and extremities, chills, and sweats. If I saw someone in my condition, I too would say poison."

"Do you have any idea what kind?" asked Flint.

Gerall shook his head and groaned at the pain that shot through him.

"We need to question Charlie," said Eloa.

Flint and Jamen shared a look.

"We've questioned him all night. He won't give up a thing," said Jamen.

Eloa's face hardened. "Let me ask him."

"No." Gerall grabbed her arm. He didn't want her anywhere near the bastard.

She looked at him, her gentle eyes softening. "I'll do it with your brothers there. He won't hurt me."

"It's worth a shot," said Jamen. "We haven't gotten anywhere."

He didn't want Eloa anywhere near Charlie, more than that, he didn't want her out of his sight.

"All right," he finally said. "But if he lays a hand on you—"

"We won't let him. Don't worry," replied Flint.

Zelle appeared in the door. "I'll sit with him."

She swept over to the bed and sat. Dipping a rag into a bowl of water and herbs, she pressed it to his forehead.

Gerall appreciated Zelle's care and concern, but he really wanted Eloa back in his arms. Especially if he didn't have much time left to hold her.

ELOA FOLLOWED FLINT AND JAMEN DOWN THE STAIRS AND out the solar door toward the stable. Her bare feet crunched over the gravel, and she looked over her shoulder back at the house. Of one thing she was entirely sure, if she couldn't find out the poison used on Gerall, he would die. From her limited study of poisons and such she knew, the longer it took to work, the worse it would be in the end. Toxins like that were only used if they were intended to be fatal and the user didn't want to be identified.

She entered the stable, her feet crackling over the hay strewn across the ground. Steeds taller and broader than she'd ever seen took up most of the stalls. She crossed the room to the end, and the brothers stopped by a door. They opened it and walked into the tack room. She followed them in, and they closed the door behind her before pulling up a trapdoor in the floor. Lanterns lit the way down a passage underneath the stable. Flint walked down the steps first, followed by Eloa. Jamen followed her, closing the trapdoor and securing it with a bolt.

"I take it no one knows about this place," she said.

"Only our family," Flint replied.

Zelle's words rang in her mind. *"Trust me, as far as this family is concerned, you are now."*

She followed the narrow stone passage until it opened into a large room. Mattresses covered the wooden floor and more weapons than she'd ever seen lined the walls. In the middle of the room, tied to a chair sat Charlie, battered and bloodied. His head lolled to one side, his tunic and breeches covered in cuts, holes, and blood. Adrian, the giant werewolf, patiently sat in the corner, wiping his bloodied hands on a towel.

"What's she doing down here?" he asked. "This is no place for a lady."

"Gerall's been poisoned." Jamen lifted Charlie's head by the hair. "And she's going to find out what kind of poison."

Charlie grunted and opened his one still-working eye to peer at her. His lips raised into a sneer and then he spit on the floor.

Jamen backhanded him, making Charlie groan.

"All right," said Flint. "Your turn."

Eloa swallowed hard. What she had planned she'd only seen her father do once in an effort to keep a wayward young man from going down the wrong path. His had been a simple suggestion. What she had planned was a lot more than that.

Eloa wiped her hands on her dress and walked to Charlie. She looked down at him and placed her hands on either side of his head. She yanked on the magick inside her and formed it into a thought, a suggestion, something enticing.

"Charlie, did you use poison on the blade you cut Gerall with?"

Charlie's eyes connected with hers, and he smiled. "Yes."

She pulled her magick harder and formed her next question, forcing a smile onto her lips.

"Tell me the poison you used."

His eyes grew glassy, and he opened his mouth, but then his gaze hardened.

"No."

She forced herself to remain calm. "You want to tell me, don't you?"

Again, his words came out hard. "No."

Frustration bubbled inside her. She licked her lips and pulled harder on her magick.

"You want to go home, don't you? Tell me the poison you used, and we'll let you go." Again, she made her voice as calm and soothing as possible, the way she'd seen her father do.

"No."

She stepped back from him and blew out a breath. Her heart raced, and her limbs shook with fatigue.

"This isn't going to work," said Flint. "We need to do something else. Something more drastic."

"Like what?" asked Adrian. "We've tried everything."

"Not everything," replied Eloa.

She'd done it only once. She'd been ten, and a girl in the village refused to stop picking on her. She hadn't even realized what she'd done until it had been too late. Her father had told her never to do it again. He'd told her it was the worst form of magick. Dark. Evil. He'd made her promise never to do it again. Using that kind of dark magick could twist her. Change her. Into what, she did not know. But to save Gerall- it was worth the cost.

Eloa stepped up to Charlie again.

He grinned up at her. "Give me your best shot, sweetheart."

Eloa reached deep inside her. Inside the place, her father would not let her go. The place where she kept all of her pain. Her loneliness. Her anger. What Charlie and Trent had done to her father. The death of her mother. The agony and fatigue of healing her father repeatedly and still it not being enough rose inside her like a tidal wave. Darkness tinged the edges of her vision and Charlie's smirk fell from his face.

She reached out with her hands and cupped his head again in her palms.

"Tell me the poison."

"No." Charlie's words came out almost a whisper.

Fear. *Good.*

Eloa unleashed her magick. Charlie's eyes popped wide as the magick pulsed through her veins and pumped into his mind. Wave after wave pulsed through her and she let it seep into his brain, clouding his thoughts, darkening his soul. His mouth opened and closed, and every muscle in his body strained against the ropes that bound him. Hotter and hotter she let her magick burn into him.

"Tell me the poison."

He bucked in his seat and pulled against the ropes. "N......ooooooo," he stammered.

"This is just a taste of what I will do," she said. "I will scramble your brain like eggs if you don't answer me."

His mouth opened in a silent scream, but he didn't speak.

Eloa pulled harder on her magick and pressed it into his mind, invading every crevasse. He screamed so loud that Eloa waited for her ears to bleed.

"Tell me," she yelled. "Tell me what the poison is!"

"I don't know!" he replied.

Flint ran to them. "What do you mean you don't know?"

"It... wasn't mine! It was... g... g... g... given to me!"

"Who?" asked Jamen. "Who gave it to you?"

"Th... th... the magistrate!"

"Is that who has Fendrick?" asked Adrian.

"Yes!"

"Where is he?" Adrian demanded.

Charlie's eyes bugged so hard out of his head that they looked like they might pop. "Storm… cellar…"

"Where?" asked Eloa.

"Flower… garden…" Charlie screamed, and blood trickled from his ears.

"That's enough." Jamen touched her arm, and Eloa let go of Charlie's head.

She took a deep breath and looked around at the men; the anger and pain still racing through her. They stared at her, no one moving, as Charlie sobbed in his chair. Finally, Flint walked to her slowly, removed his glasses, and took her hand in his.

"Thank you, Eloa."

His dead eyes searched her face. She focused her thoughts away from the anger and the pain and forced herself to lock it back where it belonged. She touched the scars around his eyes.

"You're blind," she said.

Flint didn't reply. Instead, he stood very still, letting her touch his face. Little by little, the darkness receded from her vision, and she took a deep breath and stepped away from him.

He replaced his glasses, and she watched as he blinked and looked at her again.

"We need to go," said Jamen. "We have to find the magistrate and figure out the poison."

Flint nodded. "First, we must tell Erik what's going on. He needs to come back with Hass and Ian."

Adrian grabbed Charlie's shoulders. "What flower garden?"

Charlie babbled incoherently.

"What garden?" he yelled.

Adrian raced from the room.

"Adrian, wait!" called Jamen. "You don't even know where you're going."

"Doesn't matter. I'll tear apart ever storm cellar in a garden I can find." The trap door banged open and then heavy footsteps ran overhead.

"We should go with him," said Jamen. "It could be an ambush."

"No," replied Flint. "We need to help Gerall. After Erik arrives, we'll send Hass and Ian after him." Flint held his arm out to Eloa. "Come, let's get you back to Gerall." She took it, and together they headed out of the room.

"What should we do with him?" Eloa looked back at Charlie.

They all stared at him for a moment. His head lolled to the side, his eyes glazed as if not seeing, and he continued to babble to himself.

Flint stopped. "We'll take him into the woods and let the animals have his remains. He won't last much longer."

He looked down at Eloa as if for approval. She nodded, and they continued out of the training room.

Flint walked Eloa back to the manor house.

"Can I see it?" she asked.

"What?"

"The mirror that you use to communicate with your brother?"

Flint nodded and led her through the solar into the front hall. From there, he turned into the grand hall, and they walked to the head table. Behind it, they opened the door to a small anteroom. In it sat a chair and writing table and, in the corner, stood an ornate but ordinary looking mirror.

"Where did you get it?" she asked.

"From Cinder. She found several in Ville DeFee and gave this one to us so we could keep in contact. The smaller one Erik carries belonged to Sage, my sister's husband."

Eloa watched Flint press a large red stone at the top of the mirror. The mirror's surface rippled like a pond.

"Erik Gwyn," Flint called.

The scene shifted and zoomed forward, making Eloa's stomach turn at the sight of it. Finally, the mirror stopped moving, and the surface showed nothing but darkness. Sounds of horses trotting filled the room.

"Erik!" Flint yelled.

A flash of light pierced the mirror, and then it went dark again.

"Erik!" he yelled louder.

"Whoa. Did you hear that?" asked a muffled voice.

"Hass, it's Flint. Take the mirror out of the saddlebag, you dolt!"

The horses stopped, and then the mirror flooded with light as the image lifted out of a dark bag. One of the twins' scruffy faces loomed into view.

"Heya, Flint. Get into any good fights since we've been gone?"

"Hand the mirror to Erik," Flint growled.

"No manners at all. Can't even say please?"

"Hass!"

"Give it to me," said Erik.

"Man, you two are as bossy as mom and dad were."

The mirror switched hands, and Erik's handsome face appeared.

"What's wrong?" he asked.

Flint licked his lips. "You need to come back immediately."

His expression darkened. "What's happened?"

"It's Gerall. He's been stabbed with a poisoned blade."

"What? How?"

"There isn't time. The magistrate supplied the blade. I think he's the one behind everything. He has Fendrick. We need to go in there. Now. Gerall doesn't have much time."

Erik nodded. "We're half a day's ride away."

Flint paused for a moment and looked to Eloa and then back at the mirror. "I don't know if we have that long."

Erik's expression saddened, and he looked around. "We'll head to Cinder's and come through the mirror. Keep it open."

Flint nodded, and then the mirror went dark.

"So... you go to Ville DeFee often, then?" she asked.

Flint looked at her. "Not often but—"

He looked back at the mirror. "Queen Cinder of Ville DeFee."

The mirror zoomed in and out of scenes again, landing on a large bedroom full of beautiful colors. Eloa's heart squeezed. Ville DeFee castle.

"Cinder?" Flint called.

There was a giggle and then the sound of rustling fabric.

"Cinder?" he called louder.

The noise stopped.

"My heavens, we have to move that thing out of our bedroom," said a man.

"Erik?" a female called.

"Flint."

"Can this wait?" called the man.

"Sorry Rome," Flint replied, his cheeks reddening.

Light footsteps padded toward the mirror, and a beautiful blonde woman appeared in a cream silk bathrobe. Embarrassed, Eloa turned away.

Cinder pushed at her messy hair. "Flint, to what do I owe the pleasure?"

"Gerall has been poisoned, but we don't know what with. Can you come and heal him?"

"How long ago?"

"Close to eighteen hours."

Cinder's face paled, and her eyes saddened. "I'm sorry, Flint, I can't."

"Why?"

"The poison has been in his system too long. It would take everything I have to try and find it and cure it in every part of his body. It would kill me. I'm sorry," she said quietly. "But I can come and see what I can do."

"Thank you," said Flint. "Erik and the twins are near Ville DeFee. They will need to borrow the mirror to travel back."

"Not a problem," said a man walking into the mirror frame. "I'll make sure the guards let them right through and then we'll send them along."

"Thank you, Rome."

Eloa's hands shook. The king and queen of Ville DeFee, her father's people, stood in front of her and the queen herself was coming to tend to Gerall. Her Gerall. Eloa could hardly believe it.

"Let me dress and gather some supplies, and I'll be there promptly," said Cinder.

Flint turned to Eloa and nodded. "Let's get you back to Gerall. I'm sure he's going crazy with worry."

Eloa nodded, and they headed to the door. So many questions swirled in her mind she could hardly focus. It didn't matter though; her biggest question wasn't for Flint. It was for Queen Cinder.

CHAPTER THIRTEEN

Gerall's body felt like fire burned him from the inside out. He fought to keep awake as once again, and his ribcage squeezed like he'd been set upon by his horse. Zelle continued to dab his head and hum soothingly, but he could see the troubled expression she fought to hide. He was dying, and he knew it.

"Why don't you go check on your babies," he croaked.

She gave him a tight smile and shook her head. "They are just fine with Scarlet. I'd rather be here."

Gerall took her cool hand in his now burning one. "I know you wouldn't, but I appreciate your words nonetheless."

Her chin quivered, and her eyes filled with tears. "I feel so helpless."

He squeezed her hand. "I want to thank you."

She swiped at her tears. "For what?"

"For marrying my brother."

Zelle laughed and then sucked in a breath.

"I mean it. He was lost before you. In pain that none of us could help with. I feared he would be alone forever, but you and the twins have brought life back into our family. You've given us the hope for our futures."

"You give me too much credit."

Gerall smiled at her. "You'll never know what you've done. We are all in your debt."

The door opened, and Eloa and Flint entered. Zelle stood and walked to Flint. He took her in his arms and hugged her tight. Eloa sat on the edge of the bed, her eyes filled with anguish.

"He didn't tell you anything, did he?"

"Oh, he talked," said Flint. "But he doesn't know the poison. He said the magistrate gave him the knife. Erik, Hass, and Ian should be back within the hour; then we'll head down to Westfall."

Gerall nodded. He wanted to know what Eloa had done to make Charlie talk, but the dark expression on her face told him he shouldn't ask.

"Queen Cinder is coming," said Eloa. "She should be here soon."

"Can she heal me?"

Eloa looked to Flint and then shook her head. "She said it has been too long since you were stabbed."

The blows just kept coming, and for the first time, Gerall realized he might not make it through the fight. It hadn't been since the battle with Remus and the other vampires that he'd thought of the possibility.

"Can you give us some time alone?" he asked Flint.

Flint nodded, and he and Zelle walked out. He pulled on Eloa's hand, and she lay down beside him, her skin cooling his scorching flesh. She laid her head on his chest, and he kissed her hair.

"Tell me about your life," he said.

"There isn't much to tell. I was born in the bakery and lived my whole life there until yesterday."

"So, you've never been to Ville DeFee?"

She shook her head. "My father said his family is all dead. There's nothing to go back to."

"Well, now you can. I'm sure Cinder will be more than happy to take you back with her after..." He couldn't finish his sentence. After he died, she should go back and be with the fae. Yes, his brothers would keep helping her if Gerall's wished it, but he didn't want her life to be shadowed by her few weeks with him.

"Don't say that," she said. "We are going to find a way to fix you."

"Eloa—"

"Don't!" She sat up suddenly. A tear leaked out of the corner of her eye. "Don't say it," she whispered.

He brushed the tear from her face and pulled her back to him. They lay in silence for several minutes.

"Besides," she finally said. "I can't leave my bakery."

He chuckled. "It's just a bakery."

"It's my home and—"

"And?"

Her body tensed. "And... My father is there."

Questions rolled around in Gerall's mind. "Your father? He's... not dead?"

She shook her head.

It made sense. Her not wanting him to go in the hut. Always heading back to her bakery to check on things. The fear of anyone going in.

"He's hiding," said Gerall.

"Last year, men broke into the bakery and beat my father almost to death. They left him for dead and set fire to the bakery. When I found him, he barely lived. I did my best to heal him, but my magick isn't strong enough, so he's terribly burned and scarred. I'm afraid if he's found out, they will come back and finish him off to keep him quiet."

"Why would they do that?"

"Because he wouldn't pay protection money. He refused, no matter how much they pressured him."

"Like you."

She nodded.

Anger coursed through Gerall. He wanted to rip Charlie, the others and the magistrate to ribbons for the pain they'd caused.

"We should bring your father here," said Gerall. "We'll tell my brothers when they go to town to get him and bring him back. It's possible Cinder could help him as well."

"Do you really think Queen Cinder might help?" asked Eloa.

"Think I might help with what?" Cinder stood in the doorway with Erik, Hass, and Ian. The brothers pushed past her and swarmed the bed.

"How did this happen?" asked Erik.

"Who did it?" said Hass.

"We'll kill them," finished Ian.

"We think it was Jopin," said Gerall.

"The magistrate stabbed you?" Erik's eyebrows knit together.

"No. He gave the poisoned blade to a man named Charlie."

"To stab you?"

"No..." Gerall tried to breathe deeply, but couldn't.

He began coughing again, and Cinder rushed over. Pushing his brothers aside, she opened her bag. She removed a vial and held it to Gerall's lips. He drank down the cooling liquid and then laid back. His coughing eased, and he breathed deeper than he had in hours.

The group waited for him to speak again. His eyes went to Eloa, whose face burned with shame and sadness.

"Thank you," he said to Cinder.

She nodded and laid her hands on his chest. White light grew from her palms, cooling his fevered skin. He let out an audible sigh, and his vision cleared a bit.

"Are you healing him?" asked Erik.

"No," replied Cinder. "I am pulling down the fever temporarily and clearing his lungs. Nothing will be a permanent fix at this point. Even pulling down his fever isn't the best thing to do. The fever is his body fighting the poison. But this will bring him some comfort for a while at least until we can figure out what to do."

"So, there's nothing you can do?" asked Erik.

"Tell me the poison. If you can do that, I may be able to help."

"How much time does he have?" asked Hass.

Cinder looked between the group. "It's hard to say but... less than twelve hours."

Eloa's eyes welled with tears again.

"Then we need to go," said Erik. "Hass, Ian, you and Jamen will go with me. Flint will stay here with the women and babies."

"I need you to do me a favor," said Gerall. "Go to Eloa's bakery and bring her father back with you."

"Her father?"

"It's a long story," said Gerall. "But we need him here and safe."

Erik nodded. "Of course. We can send Adrian."

"He's gone," said Jamen. "Charlie said Fendrick is in a storm cellar near a garden."

"That could be anywhere," said Erik.

"That's what we said, but he wouldn't be stopped."

The brothers headed out, and Cinder looked at Eloa, studying her for a moment.

"Half fae?"

Eloa squeezed Gerall's hand tight and then nodded.

Cinder smiled. "I'm Cinder."

"Eloa."

"Pleasure." She looked down to where Eloa held Gerall's hand. "I'm going to give you something to help you sleep."

"I don't want—"

Cinder help up her hand. "Sleeping now could buy you time later."

Gerall refused to argue. Cinder pulled another vial from

her bag, and Gerall drank it. The instantaneous effect made his muscles relax, and his mind fuzz over.

"I'm going to go downstairs and speak to Erik before he leaves," she said. "I'll come check on you in a bit."

Gerall nodded, barely able to keep his eyes open. Light footsteps headed for the door.

"Lie with me?" he asked.

Eloa stood and pulled down the covers before crawling under the blankets and wrapping her arms around him.

His mind drifted toward sleep, but before he did, he muttered. "I love you."

Eloa laid with her arms wrapped fiercely around Gerall. He loved her. He really loved her. For over an hour, she whispered that she loved him. That she needed him. She told him how she'd loved him since she'd first seen him years before. How she admired him and his kindness. How in the short time they'd been together, he had changed her life forever. She did not know if he could hear a word she said, but it didn't matter. She couldn't afford to be afraid any longer. Who knew how much time they had left. His snores deepened, making it impossible for her to sleep, so she slipped out of bed and crept to the door. Turning back, she stared at his face, again pale with deep circles under his eyes. Her chest squeezed. She hated to leave his side, but she hadn't eaten in almost twenty-four hours, and she needed to stay strong for him. Eloa slipped out the door and down the hallway. Voices floated up to meet her, and she headed for the solar. Inside, Cinder and Flint spoke in hushed voices.

"...so, I wondered if you were able to do those things," he said.

"Tell me exactly what happened," Cinder replied.

"She put her hands on either side of his head and just... I don't know... Blasted him with her magick like lightning bolts to his skull or something. His screams were almost inhuman. Whatever she did, it was painful enough that he confessed everything. Even with Jamen and I working on him for hours, he hadn't cracked."

"Was there anything else? A smell or colors or sounds?"

"When she turned toward me, her eyes were black."

"I see."

Eloa's heart pounded. Had her eyes been black? Her vision had gone dark, but she'd had no idea that they'd gone black. Her hands began to shake. That couldn't be good.

"What?" asked Flint. "You know something."

"I'm afraid... I'm afraid Eloa is dark fae."

"Dark fae? I've never heard anything about any dark fae."

"That's because as far as we knew, there weren't any left. Back when the daemons invaded Fairelle. The fae and the mages mixed their magicks to defeat them, push them back, and create the portal. That combination of magicks created the wastelands. After, some of those fae became obsessed with the immense power they'd gained combining their magick with the mages. So, they followed the mages back to the towers and studied with them to learn more. It twisted them and turned their hearts dark. Soon they were too powerful for even the mages to control. They asked our ancestors to step in and help them kill the dark fae before they became just like the daemons. We believed they'd all been killed off a thousand years ago. We must have been misinformed."

"So Eloa's father..."

"Is a dark fae. I need to find him, to talk to him and see if there are more like him. If there are, this could be bad for everyone."

Eloa's heart beat so hard she feared everyone in the house could hear it. She covered her mouth with her hand to keep from screaming. Trying to keep her breathing even, she pressed her back into the stone wall to keep from falling.

"What about Eloa? Is she dangerous?"

"Everyone is dangerous, Flint. You know that better than most. But do I think she is a danger to you and your family? From what I saw, no. She seems genuinely sweet and kind. I doubt she even knows what she is. But if you are truly concerned, you could have Zelle read Eloa's aura."

"Perhaps. I'll need to talk to my brothers."

"I could take her with me back to Ville DeFee, if..." Cinder's words trailed off, but Eloa didn't need her to finish the sentence to know what she meant.

"No," said Flint. "She is Gerall's choice. She is a Gwyn now. We'll protect her like all the others. Hell, my wife *is* a daemon. My children are half daemons. My sister and her husband are vampires. A half dark fae is nothing compared to that." He snorted. "To be honest, if she were normal, I'd be more worried than I am about her being half dark fae."

Cinder chuckled. "I see your point. I'm here for all of you if you need me. Especially her."

"Well," said Flint. "I think she'll appreciate that. Won't you, Eloa?"

Eloa's head whipped up. How had he known she stood there? Embarrassed, she looked around to find a place she could hide, but there wasn't anything nearby.

Swallowing her fear, she stepped into the doorway. "I didn't mean to pry. I just came down to find something to eat."

Flint stared at her through his sightless eyes. Cinder's expression softened.

"Come in, child." Cinder held her hand out for Eloa.

Eloa walked forward, wondering how old Cinder was to be calling her child. Her beautiful light curls hung perfectly down her back, and her bright blue eyes watched Eloa with great interest.

Flint rose and offered Eloa his chair. He stepped to the side, and she sat across from Cinder.

"I'm sorry you had to find out like that," Cinder said.

"I wish my father had told me."

"So, he never mentioned he was dark fae?"

Eloa shook her head. "He just said he left Ville DeFee after his mother and brothers died, and he traveled for a while before coming upon Westfall. He met my mother and stayed."

"Do you know your father's surname?"

"Vitalya. When he married my mother, he took her human last name to cover his fae heritage. So, I am Eloa Lenter."

Cinder nodded. "But you know nothing else of him. Why he is dark, where he came from, how he got that way?"

She shook her head. "He said his mother and brothers lived in Ville DeFee, but they're dead now."

"I would much like to speak to your father."

"Erik, Jamen and the twins went to fetch him while they are in Westfall," said Flint.

"Good," said Cinder.

"I know he is... what you say he is, but I can promise you, your highness, that he's never been anything, but gentle and kind to everyone." Eloa couldn't forgive her father for lying to her about what they were, but he was a good man, no matter what kind of magick he had.

"I believe you. To raise a daughter such as you, he'd have to be. But did he ever hint at anything about the dark fae or dark magick? Did he ever teach you anything?"

"Once I harmed a girl in town. He told me never ever to use my magick like that again. That it was wrong. He taught me how to use it to make my baked goods taste better, and I can do light healing, but not much else, I'm afraid." Eloa looked at her hands, dreading the question that had been bubbling inside her. "Are you... going to kill my father?"

Eloa raised her gaze, and Cinder sat quietly for a long moment. "If he is what you say he is, then I see no reason to bring him before the tribunal. But it is imperative that I speak to him. We must know if there are more and if so, where they are."

Eloa nodded.

"And you must be careful, Eloa. That kind of magick is

enticing and seductive. You must never use it again, or you risk it consuming your light forever."

"I understand."

"Why don't you eat," said Flint. "There is plenty of food in the kitchen. Then get some rest. I'll let you and Gerall know when Erik returns."

Eloa nodded and headed into the kitchen. She stared at one of her loaves of bread. She was a dark fae. Her magick was partly evil. She remembered the feel of hurting Charlie. The power, the way she liked it. Her stomach roiled like she'd eaten rotten meat. She had to talk to her father. She needed to know who they were and why he hadn't ever told her the truth. But above all... she had to tell Gerall. He'd asked her to marry him, but he hadn't known what she was when he'd asked. Her sour stomach intensified at the idea that he may no longer want her.

She blew out a breath and left the kitchen no longer hungry. She walked back up the stairs and slid into Gerall's room. Crawling under the blanket with him, she hugged his feverish body. The information could wait until he healed. Telling him now would only add to his torment.

CHAPTER FOURTEEN

Voices floated up the stairs awaking Eloa. She looked at the clock to find it close to ten p.m. Lights swam through the crack in the open bedroom door, and it sounded as if everyone had returned.

She looked at Gerall, whose body blazed hotter than ever. His breathing had become so shallow she knew there wasn't much time left for him. She laid her head on his chest, and his heartbeat thundered beneath his ribs. Her chest squeezed. She couldn't lose him. Not now.

She shook his shoulder. "Gerall? Can you hear me?"

He moaned, and his eyes fluttered open but closed again.

"Wake up, darling, please. Tell me what to do. How do I fix you? Don't leave me. I can't lose you."

His eyes opened slowly, and he sucked in a ragged breath and whispered something she couldn't hear.

"What?" She leaned in close, pressing her ear to his lips.

"Snow."

"Snow? You want your sister?"

"Snow... help... me..."

How could his sister help him? She didn't have time to think about it. Instead, she dashed to the door and down the stairs where the entire household had gathered in the front hallway.

"Did you find the magistrate and my father?" she asked.

The brothers looked at each other and then shook their heads.

"Neither," replied Erik. "The magistrate and his wife were both gone and their house dark. We waited as long as we could, but were told they'd left yesterday. We couldn't get into your bakery. And all things considered, we figured it might be better if we didn't force our way in. We weren't sure how your father would react."

She nodded. "Plus, I magicked the entire building."

"Is Gerall awake?" asked Jamen.

"Barely. His chest hardly moves to breathe."

"Then there is nothing left to do," said Flint.

An air of anguish suddenly subdued the entire room.

"I'm going to kill him." Flint burst from the front hall and ran through the solar.

"Flint!" Erik yelled.

Hass and Ian ran after Flint as he burst through the door and headed to the stable.

"Wait!" Eloa tried to get Erik's attention. "Gerall said something. He said Snow could help him."

"Snow?" asked Erik.

"No," said Jamen. "Flint would—"

"Flint would do it if it would save his life. Just like with Snow. He'll come around."

"This isn't smart," said Jamen.

"You have no choice," replied Cinder. "Unless you want Gerall to die. Call your sister. Turn him into a vampire. It's your only option."

A vampire? Eloa's heart thundered. That's how they fixed Gerall? By turning him into a vampire? She tried to wrap her mind around it. What would he become? Dark? Twisted? Bloodthirsty? Guilt ran through her. How could she even worry about him turning into something like that when she had evil coursing through her veins?

"Do it," she said. "If it's what he wants and it's the only way, then do it. I'd rather have a vampire for a husband than no Gerall at all."

Erik and Jamen shared a tense moment, and then Erik nodded. "Call her. I'll tell the others."

The brothers parted, leaving only the women standing around her. A week ago, all she'd had to worry about was hiding her ears. Now she had a whole myriad of secrets to hide, and the majority were not hers.

"It'll be all right." Zelle took her hands. "I know you're scared, but becoming a vampire won't change who he is. There will be an adjustment period, but you'll have all of us to help you. Whatever either of you need."

Eloa nodded, and the women pressed in around her, hugging her tight.

"You're not alone anymore," said Scarlet. "Don't worry."

The affection of the women both soothed and smothered her. She'd never had friends before, let alone a family.

Soon footsteps ran through the great hall toward them. The women backed up, and Eloa gasped as Snow, skin like pale stone, appeared in a blood-red gown, her dark hair flowing wildly around her. And at her side, a man just as pale with long blond hair and bright, sharp eyes.

Without a word, they ran past the group and up the stairs. Jamen grabbed Eloa's hands and pulled her with them, the rest of the women close behind. More yelling followed, and soon Hass, Ian, Erik, and Flint raced up too. When Eloa entered Gerall's room, Snow sat on the bed bloody tears falling down her cheeks. She whipped around and quick as light slapped Erik.

"How could you not tell me? How could you!" she yelled. "Did you think I didn't deserve to know?"

The man came up behind her and wrapped his arm around her shoulder. "Easy, Love. They're hurting too."

"I'm sorry," said Erik. "It all happened so fast."

Snow burst into tears and turned into her husband's chest.

"Eloa," Gerall's voice came out weak and soft. He held his hand out to her, and she crossed to him, sitting on the edge of the bed.

"I'm here." She picked up the rag and dabbed his head.

"You... understand... what... Snow—"

"You want her to turn you." Eloa's hand warmed at the slightest touch of his fevered brow.

Gerall nodded. "I... want... your... blessing..."

"You don't need my blessing,; you need to make this decision for yourself. It's your life."

"Our... life..."

"Our life." It wasn't lost on Eloa that the entire room had gone silent. Everyone waited for her decision. A decision of life or death for another human being. A man. The man she loved and wanted to be with. "I would rather have you than not have you. But you must decide this for yourself. I cannot do this for you."

Gerall searched her eyes and then nodded. Turning his head slightly, he looked at the group. "Snow."

She rushed forward and took his hand, kneeling on the floor beside the bed. "I'm here. I'm here."

Snow's husband joined them. Gerall looked up at them. "Do... it..."

Snow nodded and bit into her wrist. She held it over Gerall's mouth, and Gerall drank down the dark oozing liquid. After a minute, Snow removed her wrist and sealed it shut with a lick.

Eloa looked at Gerall and waited. She waited for him to do something. For the color to come back to his cheeks. For him to sit up and smile. Anything. But he didn't.

"I don't understand," she said. "Why didn't it work?"

"It will work," said Sage. "But first, he must die. We can wait, or..."

"No," said Eloa. "We... we can't just kill him."

"We aren't," said Snow. "We're giving him a new life."

"Do it," said Gerall.

"No," replied Flint. The brothers held him back.

Gerall looked to Flint. "It's what I want."

"It's not what you want," Flint said. "It's what you've got."

"Look at me," said Snow, getting to her feet. "Am I really so bad that you wouldn't want Gerall to be like me?"

"You know that's not what I mean," he replied.

"Isn't it?"

"Come," said Zelle. "Let's go check on the twins." She took Flint by the arm and led him from the room. It amazed Eloa that such a tiny, demure woman could have so much sway over such a hulk of a man.

"I'll do it," said Sage. "Quick. Painless. And then he'll come back, and he can move on with his life."

"We can't just turn into vampires every time one of us is going to die," said Hass.

"Why not?" asked Ian. "It's like having a second chance. Defying death. I love it."

Hass shook his head.

Snow stood and took Sage's hand. "I'll stay with you."

He kissed her forehead. "No, Love. You shouldn't see this. You go with your brothers. He'll need to feed quickly after turning so if you could arrange that—"

"We are all here," said Hass.

"He can drink any of us," finished Ian

"Let's clear the room." Erik looked at her. "You, too."

She looked at Gerall, and he nodded. "You... shouldn't... see... this."

She bent over and kissed his fiery lips. "I'll be here for you when you wake."

He wrapped an arm around her and kissed her hard. "I love you."

She smiled and wiped her fallen tears from his face. "I love you too."

Snow took her hand and led her from the room. Gerall's eyes never left hers until Snow closed the door.

Eloa's entire being ran cold.

"Why don't we get some tea?" said Snow. She threw Eloa a tight smile, holding her hand so tightly that she wasn't sure if it was to steady Snow, or herself.

Snow nodded and then led Eloa from Gerall's door. Eloa looked over her shoulder and her mind flooded with terrible images of what Sage was doing to Gerall at that moment.

"That dress fits you nicely," said Snow. "I'm glad that you and my other sisters are getting use of them and not just letting them hang in the closet and turn to dusty rags."

"He's not going to be in pain, is he?" Eloa asked, not even noticing her dress

Snow's eyes softened as she led Eloa down the stairs. "Not at all. Sage loved Gerall as we all do. I feel terrible for my poor husband. I've asked a lot from him."

GERALL FOUGHT TO KEEP HIS EYES OPEN, BUT THEY BURNED like someone had poured acid in them. Sage looked down at him with pity.

"Just so we're clear. I don't want to nor will I derive any pleasure from doing this," he said.

"Better you than my brothers. Or Snow," Gerall replied.

"You understand what this means. There will be no more outings in the daytime— no more walking among humans without thirsting for their blood. You will have to keep vigilant every time you are around your brothers, your niece, and nephews, even the one that sat here holding your hand. This is not a thing to take lightly, Gerall."

Gerall opened his mouth to reply, but Sage held up his hand.

"But even so, even as hard as this will be for you, of all of Snow's brothers, I believe you have the best temperament to succeed in the change."

Well, that was something. It didn't matter anyway, though. He would rather have one more week with Eloa only to have her tell him she couldn't bear to be with him as a vampire, then to die and leave her so soon.

"Do. It."

Sage nodded. He leaned in close and pushed Gerall's head to the side. "Close your eyes."

Gerall closed his eyes, and a sharp pain pierced his neck. He grabbed the sheets and clung to them as blood ebb out of his body. First, his toes began to cool. Then the sensation traveled up his legs to his torso. His fingers tingled, his pounding heart slowed, and the burning left his arms and chest to be replaced with a shard of ice in his torso.

Sage reached up and grabbed Gerall's head between his palms. "Forgive me, Snow."

Gerall's head cracked to the side and then... nothingness.

TEN MINUTES LATER, A SLOW SET OF FOOTSTEPS DESCENDED the stairs. Eloa and Snow turned and looked into the hallway. Sage emerged, a trickle of blood running down his chin. His eyes were vacant and lost. Snow rose and went to him, wrapping him in her arms. He hugged her mechanically.

"Forgive me," he said.

She stepped back and cupped his face in her palms. "No. Forgive me. I should never have let you bear that burden."

He stared at her for a long moment. "I need to go home."

Snow nodded. "We'll go right now."

Eloa got to her feet. "But what about Gerall?"

Snow turned to her. "It will be several hours at least before his change is complete and he wakes. I'll be back before then."

Eloa watched as Snow and Sage disappeared around the corner.

With the Gwyn brothers congregating in their rooms and the wives tending to their young, Eloa suddenly found herself completely alone.

Several hours. It would be several hours before he woke. It gave her time. She had a good idea where she thought her father might be. She could get there and back in less than two hours. And when she returned, she'd be able to give Cinder the answers she'd been searching for.

Eloa rushed up to Snow's room and threw open the door. Striding to the closet, she rummaged around inside until she found a pair of shoes and slipped them on her feet. They were a tad too big, but they'd work. Then she slipped on a cloak and fastened it around her neck.

She headed back down the stairs and through the front

hall to the door.

"Where are you going?"

Eloa spun to find Cinder standing in the entrance to the great hall.

"To find my father."

"But Gerall—"

"Will still be d- sleeping when I return. I won't be long."

"Eloa, I don't think—"

"I can get you the answers you seek."

"In light of everything, I think that can wait."

"Can it? When Gerall wakes, I have to tell him what I am. I can't do that unless I know for myself."

"You are Eloa. The woman he loves. Same as yesterday and the day before."

"But am I? I used that magick and ever since all it has done is beg me to use it again. I feel it inside. Swirling. Growing. Wanting to be unleashed. And I want to unleash it. If I don't find out what I am and how to control this magick one day, not in the too distant future I will unleash it, and I am afraid if I do that, I'll never come back from it. So please, do me this favor. Stay with Gerall until I return."

"Will you return?" Cinder asked.

"Only death could keep me from him." Eloa opened the door and stepped out into the fresh night air. She breathed deeply and then ran down the drive.

Eloa's legs ached from the walk as she headed down the lane into eerily quiet Westfall village. Eloa glanced around, but most people had already retired at the late hour. She sighed at the sight of her bakery. The lights remained off inside, and nothing seemed amiss as she crossed the front window and headed to the hut in the back. The covered windows showed not a spec of light from within. For a moment, she wondered if her father had run from Westfall. But where would he go?

Eloa walked up the small porch and used her magick to unlock the door. Inside, her father lay on his bed in the corner. A tiny fire flickered in the smoldering ashes in the fireplace. She closed the door and then lay her cloak over the back of a chair.

"Papa." She shook his shoulder. "Papa."

He woke with a start and rolled over, brandishing a knife. Eloa backed up a pace as he blinked at her and then recognition dawned on him.

"Eloa my child." He pulled her into a hug. "Where have you been?"

"With Gerall and his brothers. He was injured, saving me from Charlie."

"Charlie? Did he hurt you?"

"No. But Gerall... he was poisoned."

"I am so sorry, Eloa."

"The Gwyn brothers came to find you but couldn't get in, so I came to get you."

"You sent them?"

"Yes. Queen Cinder of Ville DeFee is at their home. She would like to speak—"

"No. No. I cannot speak to her."

"But why?"

"There are things. Terrible things in my past. Things you don't know."

"That you are dark fae?"

His expression drooped with sadness. "I should have told you sooner. I tried to warn you. Tried to tell you not to use that magick..."

"Papa, how did you become dark fae? I don't understand. They died out a century ago."

He nodded. "They did. But I was in the library one day studying, and I came across a book. I didn't realize what it was at the time, but soon I figured out it was a history of the dark fae. How they came to be after mixing their magick with the mages. I was stupid and young and intrigued. So, I left Ville DeFee and went to the mages. I didn't tell them I was Fae. I hid my ears. I studied with them for close to a year before they found me out. I ran before they could kill me. But with nowhere to go I went the only place I could, home. For a few weeks, my mother was so happy to have me home that she couldn't see the change in me. My brothers did, though. One night they cornered me and beat me into telling them where I'd been. So, I showed them where I'd been and what I had learned." His voice trailed off as he stared at the floor.

Eloa's chest squeezed so tight she feared it might crush her heart. "You killed them," she whispered.

He nodded but didn't meet her eye. "I hadn't meant to, but the magick took over. I then realized what I'd become. I ran that night and never went back. It's a capital offense to use dark magick. And a capital offense to be a dark fae."

"You should have told me," she said.

"What good would it have done to have you angry at me? Scared of me? Scared of yourself?"

"I am scared. Scared because I have a power you did not explain to me. Powers I was unaware I even possessed. Unaware that I could-"

His eyes widened. "Eloa, what did you do?"

"Nothing."

"Tell me."

"I said I did nothing."

He jumped to his feet and grabbed her arms. "You're lying."

GERALL'S SKIN PEBBLED AS IF HE'D PLUNGED IN AN ICY POND. Every inch of him should be shivering, but surprisingly, it didn't bother him. He opened his eyes to find everything around him in crystal clear focus, although he wasn't wearing glasses. He inhaled deeply and caught the scents of everyone in the house. He smelled their scents, their sweat, and the flavors of their blood.

His stomach growled with hunger. A pain shot through him, up his throat, burning it from the inside. He sat up and hopped to his feet- the wound in his gut nothing more than a memory. Every fiber of muscle in his body moved tighter, lighter, and ready for action. He took in his room. Out of the corner appeared a beautiful, golden-haired woman.

"Cinder. Where's Eloa?"

She walked forward slowly. "You shouldn't have woken for several more hours. Let me get your sister. She just went to talk to your brothers." Cinder's steady steps headed for the door.

In a flash Gerall stood in front of her, making Cinder's eyes widen in surprise. Her fingers twitched, and sparks of magick flicked off them.

"Where is Eloa?" he asked again.

Cinder's pulse skipped, and fear wafted off of her. She backed up half a pace.

"I told her I would stay with you until she returned. She's only supposed to be gone another hour. But like I said, you weren't supposed to wake yet and—"

"Where is she?" he demanded. Anger pulsed through him, heating his thoughts and clouding his vision.

"She went to Westfall to find her father."

"Westfall? Alone?"

Cinder nodded.

"And my brothers let her go?" he boomed.

"Your brothers didn't know until after she left. The magistrate is missing, so we didn't-"

Footsteps pounded up the stairs and down the hallway. Gerall scanned the room in a flash, grabbed his tunic, and jumped through the glass window before the door opened. For a second his body soared through the air and then he landed on the gravel below. Above him, his brothers yelled for him to stop, and Snow screamed his name, but he didn't care. He only cared about Eloa and what might happen to her going into town alone.

Gerall took off down the drive running faster than he thought possible. He whipped his tunic over his head and continued onward. He breathed deep, barely catching her scent on the wind. He had to find her. Find her and make her his.

CHAPTER FIFTEEN

Eloa pulled away from her father. "What's come over you?"

"Don't you understand?" he said. "They kill dark fae. If you've become dark, we have to run."

"I'm not going anywhere."

"Did anyone see? Does anyone know?"

"The Gwyns and Queen Cinder, but they won't tell."

"You can't take the chance. I can't take the chance. We must leave."

"Leave and go where?" she asked. "We have no money, no family, nothing."

He licked his lips. "There's a place."

"What place? You always said you had nowhere you could go."

"A place for fae like us."

Eloa's heart thundered. "You mean... dark fae."

He nodded. "After I ran from Ville DeFee a second time,

I found them. Or rather they found me. They will take us in. Now come, pack only what you need. We must hurry."

He moved about the hut grabbing a small bag and stuffing various items into it.

"Papa, where are they? The dark fae?"

"It's too complicated to explain. Gather your things, and I'll tell you on the way."

Panic swept through her watching her father's frenzied actions.

"I can't go with you," she said.

"Of course, you can. "They don't care that you are only half-fae. They will welcome you as they welcomed me."

"No. I mean, I won't go with you. Gerall needs me. We're to be married."

Her father scoffed. "Married?"

"Yes. Before he... fell ill he asked me to marry him."

"But you said he was poisoned. Surely, he'll die soon. Better you leave him to his fate and come with me and secure yourself another who will provide for you."

"I can't. I... I love him."

Her father stared at her for a moment. "And are you willing to die for that love? Because that's what they'll do when your dark fae side takes over, and you can't control it. They will kill you."

"You don't know the Gwyns. They've changed."

"Humans never change. Fae never change. Why do you think after all these years I've still had to stay hidden? Because people don't change."

Gerall wasn't like that. At least, he wasn't before. Now she didn't know what he would be.

"I'll help you pack," she said. "But I'm not leaving with you father. I'm sorry."

"Eloa—"

"You heard her; she isn't leaving." Gerall stepped into the hut. His skin had taken on an alabaster tone making his eyes that much brighter. His jawline had chiseled, and his glasses were nowhere in sight.

Eloa took him in for a moment. The air that surrounded him humming with power and strength.

His gaze traveled to her, and he held out his hand. She tentatively took a step toward him.

"No." Her father yanked her back. "He's been turned. He's a vampire."

Eloa slipped from her father's grasp, her gaze never leaving Gerall's face. "I know."

She walked to Gerall and slid her hand into his cooler one. He gripped it tight and drew her into his side.

Half a dozen horses stopped and whinnied outside. Gerall sniffed the air and his eyes trained back on Eloa's father.

"We're leaving, and I suggest you do the same. My brothers have just arrived with Cinder."

Her father looked past Gerall, then ran to his bed and dragged a large object out from under it. Eloa stared in disbelief. She'd never even known he stored anything under the bed. Her father whipped a sheet from it and pressed a red stone at the top.

"Home." Without waiting, he jumped into the mirror.

"No!" Eloa ran at the mirror.

"*Abirious*!" a voice yelled from inside.

Gerall grabbed her around the waist and rolled her away, shielding her with his body as the mirror exploded, raining glass over the room.

The door burst inward, and the Gwyns stood weapons at the ready, staring at the scene. Eloa's breathing came in erratic bursts. Gone. Her father had jumped into a mirror and vanished. He'd left her. She looked up at Gerall, who gazed at her sympathetically but strained.

"I'm sorry," he said.

Eloa sucked in a shuddered breath and hugged him tight. His cool skin permeated her body.

"Gerall," said Erik. "Let her go."

"You think I would hurt her?" Gerall's arms wrapped around her tighter.

"No, I don't. I just think that this is new for everyone and we'd all feel a little bit better if you came home with us."

"Not without, Eloa."

"Of course not." Snow stepped between her brothers, pushing them out of the way. "As long as Eloa is comfortable with that, no one is going to keep her from you."

Snow's gaze connected with Eloa's, and she could see the question in her eyes.

"I have nothing holding me here anymore." Eloa linked her fingers with Gerall's. "Let's go home."

He took a step forward, and the brothers backed up. Only Snow stood her ground.

The group walked out of the hut. The brothers tense and unsure, Snow confident and at Gerall's left side, with Eloa at his right.

All around them, Westfall slept as they made their way toward the street where the horses waited like grim reapers of the night.

Hass and Ian arrived from between two houses. "We couldn't find Adrian."

"He might have already gone back to Wolvenglen."

"Let's get Gerall home and then we'll send someone to make sure." Erik pulled his steed forward. "You and Eloa take my horse. I'll ride with Jamen."

Gerall nodded and took the reins. He helped Eloa onto the horse and then turned it around. He looked around the village and breathed deeply.

"Come," said Eloa. "I'm exhausted."

Gerall put his foot in the stirrup and then heaved himself up. He went to flip his leg over the horse and stopped. His head whipped around.

"What is it?" she asked.

Gerall jumped from the horse in a flash and ran flat out toward the church.

"Shite." Erik and Jamen jumped from the back of their horse and chased after Gerall, but Snow moved fastest. A scream rang out in the church, then another, and another. Hass and Ian raced for the church as a chill swept over Eloa. Lights turned on in several huts behind businesses that lined the streets.

Not good.

Gerall grabbed the magistrate from where he hid in Father Ohana's storeroom and flung him into the chapel. Magistrate Jopin scrambled away on his hands and knees.

"You tried to kill me," Gerall said.

"My Lord, I promise you I did not."

"Charlie said you gave him the poisoned blade that he stabbed me with."

"I... I don't know what he's talking about."

Gerall's anger flared deep inside him. He leapt on the magistrate, pinning him to the ground.

"Please, stop!" the magistrate's wife cried.

"I can smell your fear. Your lies are like burnt ash on my tongue. Tell the truth, and I might let you live."

"I- I- I did give Charlie a knife, but I didn't know it was poisoned. It wasn't mine. It was given to me."

"By whom?"

"The man who wants the Gwyns out of Westfall told me if I helped him, I would be able to take your place as Lord."

Gerall grabbed Jopin by the collar. "Who?"

"He'll kill me."

Gerall's fangs descended into his mouth. "I'll kill you if you don't."

Eloa rushed to Gerall's side. "Gerall, let him go."

"For the sake of the gods tell him," yelled Mrs. Jopin.

"It was—"

A flash of light burst into the room blinding Gerall. He dropped the magistrate to the ground and covered his eyes. A strangled scream emanated, and then the light dimmed. On the floor, Jopin and his wife writhed in pain.

Eloa tugged Gerall away. “What is it? What’s doing that?”

Cinder pushed through the crowd. “Magick.”

The Jopins foamed at the mouth. Cinder ran to them and placed her hands on their chests. The couple’s eyes bugged out of their heads, and then their tongues turned black.

“Can you do anything?” asked Gerall.

Cinder closed her eyes and concentrated. “I… I can’t stop it. It’s not fae magick.” She opened her eyes and looked at Erik. “It’s... Something else. Something older.”

Finally, the Jopin’s forms shriveled, and they lay still on the floor. Dead. Cinder stood and backed away from them.

Silence permeated the room.

Finally, a shriek rang out, and the group turned to find a crowd of villagers standing in the doorway. Murmurs and fearful whispers spread across the throng.

“Move aside, please. Move aside.” Father Ohana pressed into the church. He looked between the dead bodies and the crowd inside. His gaze finally landed on Gerall.

“Vampire,” he said. “You did this. You killed them.”

“No,” said Gerall. “I didn’t.”

Father Ohana looked at Snow. “And you, a vampire as well.”

Snow stood soundly, not bothering to deny it.

He turned on Cinder. “A fae. And that one, Eloa, the baker’s daughter, a dark fae.”

Gerall wrapped a protective arm around Eloa’s shoulders.

The murmurs grew louder around the villagers.

"All of you," said Father Ohana. "Abominations to the Lord. When I buried your brother Kellan in a secret ceremony, I knew there was something off with the Gwyns, but I never imagined that you had fallen so far."

"That's enough," said Erik. "We are the Lords of these lands, and you have no right to speak to us so."

"I have every right. I speak for the people of this village. For my parishioners who look to me for guidance. What have you done for Westfall?" He looked to the crowd outside. "Look what has become of the Gwyn family and decide for yourselves. Do you want to be ruled by immortal men who have fallen from grace, or do you want to be ruled by the gods' words?"

Erik advanced on Father Ohana. "You are done in Westfall. As of this day, you and your church are no longer supported by the Gwyns. Your church will be closed, and you are to move on."

"No," said someone in the crowd. "You can't do that. You can't remove the gods from Westfall."

"The gods left Westfall a long time ago," replied Flint. "What this man peddles is no more than falsehoods and slavery."

"Blasphemy," said someone.

"Blasphemy," cried another.

Soon the entire crowd chanted the word, louder and louder with Father Ohana standing smug as ever.

It's him, thought Gerall. *Father Ohana is the one behind all of it.*

"Enough," Erik yelled. "We are Lords of this land, and if you wish to stay here, then you will go back to your homes and forget this false religion. Otherwise, you may leave with him."

Snow stepped forward and lay her hand on Erik's arm. "Brother, maybe we should think about this."

Erik pulled away. "I am Lord Gwyn of Westfall and as I say, so shall it be. I will not be ruled by peasants and charlatans." He turned to Father Ohana. "You have until morning to leave. We will be back to make sure you have."

A series of screams pulled their attention to the door. The crowd scrambled outside as Erik and the others pushed their way through to the street.

In the middle stood two enormous wolves. The larger of the two limped slightly as he made his way toward the emaciated looking gray wolf.

"That must be Fendrick," said Hass.

"Doesn't look so good," finished Ian.

Fendrick spotted the gathering crowd and growled. He bared his teeth and the hairs on his neck raised. Adrain moved forward, and Fendrick's head swung toward Adrian as if Adrian had said something.

"We should do something," said Gerall.

"Yes," announced Father Ohana. "Do something."

"Kill them," someone yelled.

"Get a pitchfork," called another.

"No!" Erik commanded. "Leave them be." He stepped between the crowd and Adrian.

"So you Gwyns are the reason there are wolves in our town. Look at them, ready to tear us apart," Father Ohana continued.

"Shut it," yelled Jamen. "King Adrian would never hurt anyone."

"Another friend of yours?" someone yelled.

A large man with a club stepped forward.

Gerall pushed Eloa behind him, and she grabbed onto the sleeve of his tunic. Gerall tensed, and his gums ached. The scent of so many people had his throat burning and ready to drink them all dry.

"Everyone should go home," said Erik. "We can handle this." He tried to motion people to disperse, but no one moved.

Adrian continued toward Fendrick who looked between the man with the club and Erik.

The man with the club took a step forward and raised the club above his head. "You can't protect us anymore. Only the gods are on our side now."

Others in the crowd agreed, and Father Ohana began to recite a verse. Fendrick growled as the group moved slowly forward.

"Stop!" commanded Erik. Jamen, and the twins, as well as Snow, formed a barricade between the crowd and the wolves.

Cinder marched forward. "Do not do this. Don't you people have any decency? Your Lords have given you a command."

"Are they your Lords?" asked Father Ohana. "Are these heathens the ones you want ruling your country?"

The man with the club tensed and then ran straight at Erik. Gerall flew to Erik's side, grabbed the man, and tossed him across the road. Fendrick growled as the man with the club landed near him and then jumped to his feet. He took a step toward Fendrick, but Adrian snarled and lunged at the man, and the man turned and ran at Adrian. He swung at Adrian, and Fendrick jumped on the man's back, knocking him to the ground. A woman screamed, and the crowd backed up as Fendrick ripped the man's throat out. Suddenly the air around Adrian shimmered, and in a flash, he resumed his human form. He grabbed Fendrick around the middle and lifted him off the downed man.

"Fendrick, stop. Stop!"

Fendrick clawed and gnashed at Adrian.

Erik tried to step in, but Adrian warned him to stay back. Adrian fell backward, still holding on to Fendrick and then rolled on top of him.

"Fendrick, calm yourself. No one is going to hurt you. I've come to take you to Hanna."

The wolf stopped thrashing.

"Hanna. You want to get back to Hanna and your children."

Fendrick whined.

"Let's go home. Brother. It's over. You're safe."

Fendrick's shape shifted and elongated into a man. "Mmmmmmy.... Ccccchhhhhildren."

"They're safe. The men didn't hurt them."

Fendrick's body shook as he began to sob.

Erik turned to the crowd. "Magistrate Jopin and one of his constituents kidnapped this man from his family. They brought him here. Beat and starved him. Do I know these men? Yes. They are close friends of our family and Fendrick did what was necessary to protect his brother and king,

Adrian. You here tonight can spread the word. The Gwyns have friends all over Fairelle. Friends that will not hesitate to defend us from any threat to our position."

Gerall scanned the crowd for Father Ohana and spotted him toward the back of the group, looking on,

"Gwyns have ruled Fairelle for over one hundred years, and we won't be bullied or removed from our duty by a few power-hungry ruffians. All the protection payments will stop, as well. If anyone in Westfall is seen pressuring shopkeepers for money, they will be hung for treason."

A murmur sounded around the crowd, and several people clapped. Gerall kept his eyes on Father Ohana as he crept back toward the church.

"Go now," said Erik. "We will take care of this. But spread the word. There will be no more falsehoods. No more charlatans. No more shake downs. No more bribes. The Gwyns will not tolerate any more oppression of those in our charge."

Gerall held out his hand to Eloa who had huddled near Cinder. She raced to him, and he kissed her head as she wrapped her arms around his waist.

The crowd slowly dispersed and Jamen walked to Adrian, draping a cloak around his shoulders. Hass pulled off his tunic and held it out to Fendrick.

"No… thank you. I don't need it."

"You run home," said Adrian.

"You… you aren't coming?"

"I'll catch up in a minute."

Fendrick licked his lips and looked at the dead man on

the ground. "I… didn't mean to… He attacked you and I just couldn't-"

Adrian touched his forehead to Fendrick's. "It's all right brother. You saved me."

"Hanna won't like it."

"She will understand. You hurry back to her. You've been gone so long, and she is desperate to have you home."

Fendrick nodded. "Hanna." He transformed in an instant and flipped to his feet. Adrian let go of him, and Fendrick took off toward the woods.

"Where did you find him?" asked Erik.

"Under the magistrate's garden in the storm cellar."

"Was there a girl there? A vampire girl?"

Adrain shook his head. "I'll be able to find out more in a few days when Fendrick has calmed down a bit."

Erik nodded.

Adrian handed the cloak back to Jamen. "I should go. I don't want Fendrick getting any ideas of coming back to get revenge."

Erik and Adrian shook hands, and then Adrian dropped to all fours, transformed and raced off.

The brothers gathered around the dead man.

"What should we do with this one?" asked Hass.

"Take him with Charlie and dump them together," said Jamen.

Hass and Ian headed to the horses and gathered them up.

Gerall pushed the hair from Eloa's face. "Are you all right?"

She nodded. "Where's Father Ohana?"

Gerall whistled to Erik. "Priest is gone."

Jamen ran to the church as the twins arrived with the horses. Gerall helped Eloa up and then mounted behind her, wrapping his arms around her waist.

Jamen ran out of the church. "He's not in there."

Erik nodded. "Good. Hopefully, he will stay gone."

"I have a feeling he was the one behind everything happening here in Westfall," said Gerall.

"If that's the case, then we most likely haven't seen the last of him," said Jamen.

"Let's get home," said Erik. "We'll come back tomorrow and board the place up after the close of Festivus."

The group mounted their horses and headed out of Westfall.

"So, you are dark fae," Gerall said. "I think there is much you and I need to discuss."

He could hear the quickening of her heartbeat.

"Yes," she said. "I suppose there is."

CHAPTER SIXTEEN

Eloa shivered in the night air as they pulled up to Gwyn manor once more. Zelle and Scarlet exited the house and waited for their husbands. Gerall pulled the steed to a stop and hopped down before helping Eloa to the ground.

"We need to talk," said Erik.

Gerall placed his hand on Eloa's back and ushered her forward. "Later."

"Gerall—"

"I said later!" he snarled.

The group fell silent.

"Gerall," said Snow. "You need to feed. The hunger is clouding your judgment and your words."

"You think I don't know that?" he spat. "I'm trying my hardest to keep it together."

Sage walked out the door. *When had Sage returned from Tanah Darah?*

Sage placed his hands on either side of Gerall's face and looked him over. Sage's voice came out calm and gentle. "Let's get you fed. It will help you see more clearly."

"I will feed," Gerall said. "But first there are some things Eloa and I need to talk about."

Tension fell thickly between them— someone needed to take charge before things got ugly.

"An hour," she said. "Give us one hour."

Though there wasn't a consensus between them, the brothers stepped aside, and Eloa walked with Gerall and into the house.

Gerall closed his bedroom door behind them and locked it. She glanced about the room and noted that nothing had changed since she'd left. Gerall walked to the window and touched it with his hand.

"Is something wrong?"

"I broke the window when I left. Cinder must have fixed it."

She wanted to ask him why the window had been broken, but there were more pressing matters at hand.

Gerall turned and strode to where she stood. "You are a dark fae?"

She nodded.

"Your doing or your father's?"

"I don't know. He was a dark fae, so I guess it passed on to me. I had only ever once used the magick before. But I cannot deny that I used the magick on Charlie to get answers."

He brushed a hair from her face. "I've read about dark fae. They say the pull of the magick is strong, enticing."

"Yes," she whispered.

"Show me."

"I... I cannot. If I do—"

"Show me what your magick can do."

Eloa didn't want to show him, but for unknown reasons, she placed her hand on his chest and let the magick flow from her palm into him. The magick made her tingle, and she fought back an audible sigh.

Gerall's hands squeezed her waist tightly, and the cords in his neck pulled taut. The desire to do more wafted through her beckoning her. *No!* She jerked her hand away. He closed his eyes and gulped for air. When he opened them again, he smiled, revealing long, white fangs.

A chill spread through her at the same time a knot of excitement furled in her belly. He'd liked it.

"Didn't that hurt?" she asked.

"Yes." His voice rang out husky and low.

Eloa licked her lips, and before she could blink, Gerall lowered his mouth to her throat. She gasped, and every muscle in her body tensed. He sniffed her, and his tongue wound its way across the vein that pounded against her skin.

"Are... you going to bite me?" she stammered.

A part of her, a dark and forbidden part wanted to say yes. But another part screamed at her to be afraid. Eloa pushed the fearful part away and stood straight. She had nothing to be afraid of. She possessed powerful magick. She wasn't some stupid farm girl who didn't know a vampire from a werewolf. Besides, this was Gerall. Her Gerall. If he'd wanted to hurt her, he could have a hundred times over in the past hours. But he hadn't. He'd held back.

"Do you want me to bite you?"

"Yes," she whispered.

Gerall's tongue stopped moving. Eloa sucked in a deep breath and held it as his fangs dragged down her skin.

"Are you sure? I don't know that I can stop if I start."

Eloa placed her palm on his chest again. "I'll stop you."

Gerall kissed her neck again, picked her up, and pinned her against the wall. Eloa wrapped her legs around his hips, and he kissed her again. Fear trembled her limbs as he licked her once more, and then his teeth pierced her skin. She let out a small cry, but then a euphoric feeling of relaxation flooded her. Gerall's mouth pulled at her neck, and a wave of pleasure flowed through her to her core. Pinned against the wall, his excitement pressed against her.

Eloa lowered her hand between their bodies and rubbed him through his breeches. He growled and pulled from her vein again.

She swirled her fingers over his chest. "Enough."

He ignored her and sucked again, but Eloa pressed her hand into his skin and unleashed a small degree of magick.

"Enough!" She pushed him away, dropping to her feet. He stared at her with an animalistic desire. He stood a foot from her, her blood dripping from his mouth. Eloa strode forward and lifted the hem of his tunic. Without speaking, he raised his arms, and she pushed it over his head and then used it to wipe his mouth. His eyes searched her face as he laced his fingers in the hair at the base of her skull and drew her to him. He bent to kiss her, but she turned her head away.

"Close my neck."

Gerall leaned in obediently and licked her throat.

"Now back away," she said.

Again, Gerall complied. She stared at him with a thrill of the control she possessed racing through her.

"Take off your breeches."

Gerall untied his breeches and dropped them to the floor. Eloa took in every inch of his long, lean body. The injury on his stomach had become barely more than a thin line, a shade lighter than his new, paler skin. Every inch of his abdomen stacked with bunched and rippling lean muscles. Not bulky like his brothers, but taut and refined.

"Lay down."

Gerall backed up until his knees hit the bed and he scooted up to the headboard and waited.

Eloa slowly untied her overdress, watching his eyes focus on each lace as she pulled them through their eyelets. After several painstaking minutes, she finally dropped the dress to the floor. She stood there, quietly mustering up the confidence to fully expose herself to him. She untied the top of her chemise and pulled it down over her shoulders. It caught on her breasts, and she tugged it to the floor. Gerall's fists wound tight in the cover of his bed, and his fangs remained elongated as he groaned. She slid her pantaloons down and then stepped out of the pile of clothing and walked to the bed.

Slowly she crawled up his body onto his lap. His cold hands ran up her legs to her arms and then down over her breasts to her waist.

She pressed her hands to his chest and pushed her face closer to his. "Kiss me."

Gerall leaned in quick, but she turned away.

"Gently."

His fingers pressed into her hips as she brought her lips to his. He swept his tongue into her mouth, and his chest rumbled. She tasted her blood on his lips as she coaxed his tongue with hers. Soon, his hands moved between her thighs, and she moaned at his touch.

He rubbed at her most sensitive parts, making her body goosebump. She arched forward, and his mouth caught her breast, and he bit it lightly, sending a wave of pleasure coursing through her. He rubbed and sucked her body, making her mind fuzz over. Then he moved her hips, so she poised above him. He pressed against her, but she pushed him back against the headboard and took charge once more.

Refusing to let him call the shots, she pressed her hand into his chest and let a small amount of magick roll out of her fingertips. He sucked in a breath, but held her gaze, intense and penetrating. She moved his hands once again to her breasts and then repositioned over him. Rotating her core across the top of him, she watched as his gaze grew more intense. His grip tightened on her, and soon he pinched her sensitive nubs, making them pucker and sending her close to an edge she didn't know she could fall over.

When she thought she might burst, she lowered herself down onto him. Inch by excruciating inch, until he filled her. Gerall sat up quickly, grabbing onto her and kissing her hard. Every part of her wanted him for herself. Wanted to surrender herself body and soul, but she couldn't. She'd seen what he'd become. She couldn't afford for him to run over her the way he'd already started to do to his family. The only way for them to survive was for her to be in charge.

She pulled her lips from his and looked deep into his eyes. She rocked her hips back and forth, their gazes never losing contact. He tried to push her faster, but she pinned his hands over his head and stopped moving.

"No," she said.

A growl escaped him, and she leaned in and kissed him softly, letting a lingering moment pass before she began to move again. She circled her hips, grinding into his and every time feeling a quake of pleasure that strummed her core. Faster and faster she moved, becoming lost in the feel of her own pleasure until finally, she dropped his hands, and he grabbed onto her hips. He kissed down her throat as her body wound tighter and closer to the edge of the bottomless cavern of pleasure.

"Look at me," he said when she closed her eyes.

He leaned back and pulled her with him, angling her body, so she slid down him completely.

"Gerall." She could barely get his name out of her mouth.

His gaze intensified. "I can't hold back much longer," he said.

"Gerall."

"Eloa, my love."

"Gerall!" Her body exploded. Every nerve ending lit like fireworks as her muscles pulled tight around him, squeezing him and pulling him deeper inside her.

"Eloa... I can't—"

"Bite me," she commanded.

In a flash, his teeth pierced her throat again. Deep and sharp, they plunged into her skin, making her body convulse with another round of climaxes. He drank from her deep, moaning, and guiding her body onto his faster and harder. Pain mixed with pleasure that she wished would never end. Soon his frenzied climax ended, and he pulled his fangs from her neck, licking her wound shut. He fell back against his headboard, and she opened her eyes to look at him once more. Her vision had clouded with darkness in the edges, and his face swam in and out of view.

He reached up and touched her face. "Your eyes are black."

"It happens when I use dark magick."

He kissed her again. "I didn't hurt you, did I?"

"No. Did I hurt you?"

"A bit." He smiled. "But I rather enjoyed it."

She kissed him hard and then looked at him again. "So did I."

GERALL COULDN'T BELIEVE THE IMMEASURABLE PLEASURE that he'd experienced with Eloa. The pain and the ecstasy merging with the blood had all brought him to heights he hadn't known were possible. The way she'd commanded him, ordered him, owned him, made him believe that they could handle what he'd become. And they'd only just begun to scratch the surface of the depths of pleasure they could bring to one another. Everything he'd learned about female anatomy had been wiped away, and like discovering a new creature, he suddenly wanted nothing more than to spend the next year in bed with her, figuring out everything that made them both tick.

But as they walked downstairs to meet with his family, he knew those things would have to wait. In the great hall, his siblings, their spouses, and Cinder awaited them. When Gerall and Eloa walked through the door, they all turned.

Tentatively, the group eyed Gerall. It pained him that they looked at him so warily. But Sage had been right. Drinking had helped him to focus.

"How are you feeling?" asked Snow.

"Better, thank you."

"Gerall, we need to talk," said Erik.

"Please," Gerall replied. "Let me go first." He looked down at Eloa, who nodded to him. Not in an eager, expectant way, as she would have two days prior, but more permitting him to say what they had discussed.

"Eloa and I have talked, and though we love being with you here in Westfall, we think it would be best if only for a short while, we retire to Tanah Darah to stay with Snow and Sage."

The group looked at each other in surprise. Sage stood from the table and walked to Gerall, laying his hand on his brother-in-law's shoulder.

"You would both be most welcome in Tanah Darah."

Gerall smiled and nodded.

"A wise decision," said Erik. "One that, though we are saddened by, we all agree is for the best. With everything we will now have to contend with here in Westfall, I no longer believe it will be a safe place for you and Eloa."

"I believe that to be true. Father Ohana will do whatever is necessary to gain control over Westfall. You must be prepared."

"So, you think Father Ohana is behind this?" asked Flint.

"Without a doubt. I saw his face when the townspeople turned against us. He was happy about it. We cannot prove it of course, and with these new miracles he has been performing, the number of believers has increased twenty-fold. For whatever reason, he is determined to take hold of Westfall."

"Then we will be even more vigilant," said Flint. "Westfall belongs to the Gwyns. It will not fall into the hands of a man spewing lies and falsehoods."

"That is a fight for another day," said Jamen. "When shall you leave?"

"Within the hour, I should think," replied Gerall. "I just need to pack a few things, and then we have one last piece of business to attend to before we depart."

"And what is that?" asked Snow.

"We need for Erik to marry us," said Eloa.

The group smiled, and all gathered around for a huge hug.

"Welcome to the family," said Erik.

"It's not too late to change your mind," said Ian.

"I'll marry you if you don't want a neckbiter for a husband," said Hass.

Eloa smiled. "Not on your life."

The End

JAK THE GIANT HEALER

FAIRELLE BOOK EIGHT

By Rebekah R. Ganiere

CHAPTER ONE

SOUTHEASTERN COAST, FAIRELLE - LATE FALL, 1213 A.D. (AFTER DAEMONS)

"You what?" Jak shouted.

"It's for your own good." Her father swayed on the spot.

"How is me being sold off in a game of cards for my own good? More likely it was for your own good." Jak slammed her fists on the rickety kitchen table making it shake.

Her father straightened his drunken shoulders. "Jakleen don't you take a tone with me-"

She stepped closer to her father, making him back up. For all of his bluster she knew the truth, she terrified her father.

"I'll take any tone I want. I am a person, not a horse, not a pig, not a chair. You cannot use me as a prize in a game of cards." She clenched her fists tight, her magic waking in her veins and begging to be used. "I will not marry that over-bearing, brainless dolt, Rupert."

"You will! Because I am your father and I say you will."

She narrowed her gaze. "Oh, you think so, do you?"

Her father's gaze flicked to the side and he licked his lips before smiling. "Rupert is popular in the village and in the last few years he has become wealthier than anyone else. He will make you a decent husband and me a respectable son in law." He clumsily reached into his pocket and pulled something out. "And he gave me this for you." Her father held out a beautiful purple and pink-jeweled butterfly hairpin.

Jak took the pin and turned it over in her hand before throwing it at her father. "Where did he suddenly get all of this wealth? Did you even bother to ask? Stealing most likely."

"You don't know that." Her father burped and steadied himself on a wobbly chair.

"And what did he promise you if you let him marry me?"

Her father straightened and pushed back his shoulders. "He promised to be a suitable husband and provider and-"

Rage flowed through Jak. She grabbed a butter knife off the table and brandished it at her father.

"All right. He... he promised to pay all my debts in town and give me a small monthly allowance."

There it was. Just as she'd said. Her father had sold her for ale and card money. Jak threw the knife across the small house where it stuck in the wall of her father's bedroom.

Her father screeched and ducked. "It was either that or sell your beloved cow, Annabelle."

"I or the cow and you chose the cow. Typical."

She couldn't believe it. Her father had always been a

wrung above pig snot but this... this was worse. Anger flared within her. How in the world could her mother have thought she'd be better off being raised by this man than with her in the forest?

Jak grabbed her shawl and wrapped it around her shoulders. She pushed passed her father and out into the early spring morning.

The sun began to peek over the hills. She kicked down the dirt path around the side of her house toward the rear. The chickens hadn't even left their nests yet and Annabelle's eyes still drooped. She shuffled to the animal and rubbed her creamy colored head.

"Sell the cow or his daughter. Not get a job. Makes perfect sense. He sees us as the same."

Annabelle continued to sleep as Jak kissed her warm head and then turned toward the road.

She walked for half a mile before arriving at the village. Only a few women were up, milking cows, feeding chickens, getting things set for the day. The scent of yeast and rising bread made her stomach growl. She wrapped her shawl tighter around herself and headed to her destination.

Jak stopped in front of the Ugly Ogre tavern and pushed open the creaky, weathered door. The pudgy owner, who resembled the name of his tavern a little too much, rubbed down the bar with a moth-ridden cloth. He stopped when he spotted her, but she paid him no mind. She glanced around the tavern. A bark of laughter flow from the back room. Jak squared her shoulders and headed for it.

"Miss," the owner called. "Miss, you can't go in there."

Another feeble attempt by a man to keep her in what he

considered her place. But she knew the men of this town all too well. Not a one possessed the guts to stand up to her.

Jak pushed through the curtain separating the rooms and the three men at the table glanced up from their cards. The two town rowdies' eyes widened at the site of her, but Rupert smiled from beneath his thick dark mustache.

"Hello, darling." He grinned

"Don't you dare call me that." She stormed to him.

"Why? We are engaged now after all." He chuckled.

The two rowdies laid their cards on the table and leisurely bee-lined for the exit, keeping a full birth as they rounded her. For once she was glad everyone in the village steered clear of her.

"How could you?"

Rupert plopped his heavy booted foot on the table. "How could I what, darling?"

The word grated on her ears like a chisel. She clenched her fists tight trying to keep control of her anger.

"I told you I wouldn't marry you last week and the month before and the month before. How could you take a bet from my father for my hand in marriage?"

"Take it from him? Darling, I'm the one who suggested the deal."

Fury pulsed through her so hard she could barely see his smug expression any longer.

"Jakleen. Why are you fighting this? No one else will take you, and your father has given you to me to be my wife. I will build you the biggest house in town. Furnish it with beautiful things and lavish you with anything you want. In return, you will adorn and love me and give me children aplenty. Why is this a bad thing?"

"If it's adoration you want, let me show you the adoration I have in store for you."

With a flick of her wrist the floorboards creaked and groaned underneath his chair. Tree roots burst through the floor knocking him over. She pushed the roots at him as he screamed and she squeezed them tight around his body. Not enough to hurt him but enough for him to realize he would never control her. She would never be his.

Wide-eyed Rupert yelled for help. He struggled against the thick roots, but they didn't budge. Jak sauntered over to him, the feel of the roots as much a part of her as if she held him in the palm of her hand.

"I will never marry you, Rupert. I will never love you. I will never adore you. If you try to force me into this marriage I can assure you, you are going to spend a lot of time pinned to the floor. And not in a way you will enjoy."

She pulled her shawl tight around her shoulders and stormed out of the room to the sounds of Rupert's continued screams. She pushed the curtain aside and stepped into the tavern. The two thugs as well as the tavern owner stared at her. Jak eyed at each of them in turn and headed to the exit.

Heavy footsteps ran into the back room.

"My toth, look what she did!"

"Get an axe, you dolts!" Rupert yelled.

Jak stepped out onto the dirt street and scanned both ways. People exited their houses at the sounds of Rupert's yelling.

She huffed down the front of the tavern the wind mixing with Rupert's screams. People drew closer to the bar, being sure to keep away from her.

"Holy mother! The old willow," a woman cried.

Jak rounded the corner, and sure enough, the old willow leaned over the top of the tavern. Its roots spread underneath the structure.

"An axe," someone yelled. "We need an axe!"

The anger inside Jak abated at the thought that they would chop up her a friend that had come to her aid. Jak moved to the tree and laid her hand on its truck.

"Thank you for your aid," she whispered.

She caressed the soft bark and bid the tree to release Rupert. The tree groaned and retreated, pulling back. Its roots slid out from under the tavern making the entire building shake. When the tree settled she touched it again, lending her strength and comfort. Jak peered up into the branches swaying though no breeze blew.

"Slumber and sleep. Drink and grow."

To read more go to your nearest retailer!

Dear Reader,

Thank you for taking the time to read *Gerall's Festivus Bride.* I had so much fun writing this book. I have loved Gerall's quiet strength for so long and couldn't wait to find him a woman of equal kindness and strength.

If you enjoyed the book, please take a moment to leave a review on your favorite retailer. Your reviews make all the difference to an author and the success of books.

If you'd like, email me and let me know what you liked about the book or who your favorite character is. I love hearing from readers. It makes writing so much more fun when I hear from my readers.

VampWereZombie@Gmail.com

To find out more about me and my Upcoming Releases, Join my Street Team for Swag and Freebies.

I also love connecting with readers! Stalk me everywhere! I look forward to hearing from you!

Rebekah R. Ganiere - BOOKS WITH A BITE

Award Winning–*USA Today* Bestselling Author

Rebekah R. Ganiere

Fairelle Series

Red the Were Hunter - Book One

Yanti's Choice - Fairelle Short Story

Snow the Vampire Slayer - Book Two

Jamen's Yuletide Bride - Book Three

Zelle and the Tower - Book Four

Cinder the Fae - Book Five

Belle and the Beast - Book Six

Gerall's Festivus Bride - Book Seven

Jak the Giant Healer - Book Eight

Wolf River

PROMISED at the Moon

CURSED by the Moon

RECLAIMED from the Moon

TAMED under the Moon

UNLEASHED with the Moon

FATED despite the Moon

The Society Series

Reign of the Vampires

Rise of the Fae

Vengeance of the Demons

The Otherworlder Series

Saving Christmas

Cupid's Curse

Kissed by the Reaper

Dracula's Bride

Rekindling Christmas

Christmas Lodge (2020)

Dead Awakenings (2020)

NEWSLETTER

To claim your Two FREE Books and find out more about Rebekah R. Ganiere and her other Upcoming Releases You can Go Here:
www.RebekahGaniere.com/Newsletter

www.ingramcontent.com/pod-product-compliance
Lightning Source LLC
Chambersburg PA
CBHW020411210626
46816CB00006BB/2225

* 9 7 8 1 6 3 3 0 0 0 5 0 6 *